I0709451

"With rebellion, awareness is born" – Albert Camus

CRITICAL PRAISE FOR
PASSAGES OF REBELLION

Fran Shor's *Passages of Rebellion* weaves a detailed, time-shifting, and enlightening account of the odyssey of an idealistic, but flawed, Frank Goodman through his student years as a 1960s radical, into his later life when he is confronted with an unexpected and deeply emotional reckoning. A good read.

Bill Harris, Detroit-based award-winning playwright and short story author

Fran Shor's fine debut novel, *Passages of Rebellion*, is grounded in actual history with dates, events, and names that will be immediately recognized by anyone with even a minimal knowledge of the response to the War in Vietnam here at home. Shor gives us an honest look at characters based on real individuals and events during that era—who bring with them all the personal and political contradictions, idealism, courage, and principles found in the student antiwar and draft resistance movement. This is a very worthwhile read.

John Marciano, independent historian and author of *The American War in Vietnam: Crime or Commemoration?*

Fran Shor has created a debut novel that not only tells the story of the birth of a radical antiwar activist through the life of Frank Goodman, but he has constructed a literary time machine back to a decade of rebellion, lost innocence, and the struggle for change and hope. Read it while listening to the raw power of Janis Joplin or wistful voice of Bob Dylan or while soaring with music of the Jefferson Airplane or The Rolling Stones and you will slip into a not so distant mirror to our times.

Marly Rusoff, a founder of the Loft Literary Center in Minneapolis

For those who haven't been on earth long enough to know, there was another period in America when the country was at least as divided as it is now. In *Passages of Rebellion*, Fran Shor reminds us in dramatic fashion about the political and cultural turmoil this country experienced during the late 1960s. Moving back and forth between those turbulent times and more recent eras, Shor crafts animated characters whose involvement with movements and events creates an illuminating mirror of the diverse passages of rebellion.

Charles Salzberg, two-time Shamus Award nominee and Beverly Hills Book Award winner

One

AUGUST 24, 1970

The telephone rang just before midnight. Barely awake, he answered mumbling, "Who is this calling so late?" It was a familiar voice; someone in the movement who knew Frank was planning on driving across the border.

"Can you take a passenger with you?"

"Who?"

"Can't tell you now, but I'll meet you with him tomorrow morning at 6 A.M. at your place."

"Okay. Just don't be any later. I want to beat the traffic and get to Canada as early as possible."

He put down the receiver, regretting that he had agreed so quickly and without questioning who this stranger was. He trusted his friend, especially since that person knew why Frank had decided now in late August 1970 to flee to Canada. Fearing potential arrest for an earlier action in which he participated with others to destroy draft files at Selective Service offices in Minnesota, Frank felt there was no alternative. He had faced imprisonment in the past, but had managed to avoid a lengthy sentence, the kind of sentence that invariably would be part of the prosecution against him and his comrades.

Only yesterday, he told Mary that he was going to "disappear." They had already split up, a wrenching separation that was about to end in divorce after signing the papers she handed him. She pleaded with him to reconsider fleeing to Canada. He hesitated while she pummeled him with arguments, based on historical and emotional ties that had bound them for over two years of momentous and frightening times. Because those times were still so resonant, they clenched each other through sobs and then slowly began a last desperate physical fusion. Weeping together as they climaxed, their bodies and their beings then separated.

No time to cry again for what was lost. Instead, Frank set his alarm for 5:30 A.M. As he descended into a fitful sleep, the memory of those early times in Minneapolis came flooding back. They washed over him as if he was re-living that past in the present.

Two

AUGUST 30, 1967

As Franklin Roosevelt Goodman turned his battered 1962 Chevy Corvair onto University Avenue, he appeared troubled. And confused. The confusion was probably attributable to the long drive from Chicago and the imprecise directions he had to reach his sight-unseen rental in a rooming house in Dinkytown. Having left his cousin's place early in the morning, he stopped to meet up with a friend in Madison. The dawdling with the latter over a lunch with a few beers and a little weed left him bleary-eyed and unprepared for the treacherous driving on the three-lane highway out of Madison. Navigating that road under the influence made for an unpleasant and paranoid drive that continued right up to the outskirts of Minneapolis, where confusion caught up with the paranoia to make the rest of the trip fraught with uncertainty.

It didn't help that the sun wasn't around to illuminate the unfamiliar city landscape. What shone in his mind's eye, however, was the re-emergence of a persistent questioning about the path he had chosen. It wasn't just second-guessing the choice of going to graduate school in American Studies at the University of Minnesota as opposed to attending Law School at the University of Michigan. Frank Goodman had also committed himself to refusing his student deferment in order to protest the draft and, more pointedly, the immoral war. That war represented everything he detested about the imperial arrogance of the country whose ritual celebration of its nationhood coincided with his birthday. Once a happy coincidence, filled with cake, ice cream, and fireworks, July 4th now reminded him that he was no longer in patriotic sync with the country in which he was born. A country, in the words of the poet bard bred further north in Hibbing, Minnesota, that believed it had "god on its side."

Maybe he should forget about grad school. Or, maybe, he should just take the damn privilege of the deferment and bury his head in the sand. And like the ostrich, bound forever to inhabit terra firma, dart to avoid the ground where corpses, both real and imagined, littered war-torn villages of Vietnam that inhabited his mind. Or, maybe, like a demon driven by the memory of those corpses, he should continue to drive straight north to Canada.

For now, a more immediate matter was finding his way to the rooming house in Dinkytown. He was sure he was heading in the right direction on University Avenue, especially since he could spot a part of the university coming up to his left. Trying to catch sight of the streets on his right, Frank pumped the brakes to indicate his tentativeness about where to turn. Ahead was a stoplight that thankfully blinked from yellow to red, allowing him the opportunity to check out the sign. He was positive that it said "4th Street," exactly where he needed to make the turn.

As the Corvair crossed over a small bridge, it entered the area known as Dinkeytown. Although Frank had seen numerous references to this lively part of Minneapolis, he had no idea what the name meant. Was it because it was such a small slice of the larger city or because it was *sui generis*, distinctive and separate from the surrounding metropolitan area? Did it have a hidden meaning that only its inhabitants and regular visitors knew and kept secret from others? In any case, the name might be revealed to him because he was about to join the ranks of its residents.

Entering Dinkytown on this warm summer night with people milling around gave Frank the feeling that he was being welcomed to his new surroundings. All he needed now was to find the next turn where he could make a left from 4th onto the street that housed the address he sought. Then, he could drop off his meager belongings and join the buoyant crowds. As tired as he was, the alluring evening buzz from the crowds on the Dinkytown streets made him eager to join in.

Turning the Corvair onto 17th Avenue, he proceeded to follow the addresses on either side of the tree-lined thoroughfare until he managed to determine which side was even and which was odd. Seeking out the exact odd number that corresponded to the rooming house address, Frank pulled the dusty and dilapidated Chevy into a vacant spot between two automobiles that looked as weather-beaten as his. He sighed in relief that he had reached his destination. The Corvair expelled a portion of its exhaust as if it too recognized it had arrived unscathed at the end of a long journey.

As Frank exited the car, he grabbed the backpack on the passenger side. There were just two pieces of bruised fruit, a brown-spotted banana and a dented green apple, neither of which appeared very appetizing when he peered in to see the remaining contents. Moving to the front of the car, which is where the trunk was in the Corvair, he opened it to retrieve one suitcase and a large duffle bag stuffed with both clean and dirty clothes, the dirty ones strategically situated on the bottom. Slinging the duffle bag over his right shoulder and grasping the suitcase in his left hand, Frank walked over to the pavement leading to the front door.

Although it was only around 9 P.M., he hesitated to ring the doorbell, fearing that he might disturb the landlady who owned the rooming house. His one previous interaction, beyond the initial letter exchange, had been a harried telephone call from a pit stop on the highway earlier in the day to let her know he would be arriving later that evening. Her obvious displeasure at the late notification and the equally "late" hour of arrival put him on guard for what might be an inhospitable beginning as a renter. Shaking off any further hesitancy, Frank extended his index finger and pushed the doorbell with purpose.

The wooden door opened slowly. Peering around the corner was a nervous looking older woman with white hair and a saggy orange-tinted face. Before Frank could speak, she forcefully inquired, "Are you that Franklin fellow who called earlier today?"

"Yes, ma'am."

"Well, you know I don't like to let folks in this late at night. And my renters have a curfew that they got to respect or I'll kick 'em out. Besides, I don't normally rent to folks like you.

Y'know, student types. Too many troublemakers nowadays. You ain't one of them troublemakers are you?"

Frank was taken aback. He was confident that his polite letter of inquiry about renting a room would have put even the most suspicious landlord at ease. That aside, he realized he would have to say something that would offset her annoyance with his late arrival.

"I'm so sorry I couldn't get here earlier in the day. It was a long drive from Chicago and I had to make a stop in Madison. I promise that I will abide by your rules and be a model renter."

"Glad to hear you say that, young man. You can come in now and I'll show you your room and tell you the other rules of the house. Please remember to address me as "Mrs. Johnson." You should know that Mr. Johnson passed a few years ago, but my older boy stops in from time to time to make sure that things are in order. He's with the Minneapolis Police. So, he's got a good eye for troublemakers."

Great, thought Frank. Not only is the landlady going to ride herd on me, but her son, the cop, could become an unwarranted and unwanted intruder into my personal and political affairs. Knowing this, Frank's steps following behind Mrs. Johnson were as plodding as hers were. When she reached the top of the stairs, she beckoned him forward into what was a combined kitchen and dining room. Waving her wrinkled right hand around the room like the wand of a surly fairy godmother, she motioned to each one of the appliances.

"That refrigerator," declared Mrs. Johnson, "is shared by all three of you renters. You need to label what's yours and make sure you don't take anything that doesn't have your name on it. I don't want to have my renters fussing and feuding over what food items they have."

Pointing to the stove, she issued another caveat. "You can cook on that stove and in that oven, but I don't want any strange smells coming from anything you cook. And, no cooking late at night! Also, make sure to clean any pot, pan, and dish you use. That also goes for silverware."

Even though Frank had worked in a dish room in a nurse's residence as an undergraduate and was not averse to cleaning up dirty pots and pans, Mrs. Johnson's tone of voice indicated he would have to be very circumspect about what he did in *her* kitchen.

Oblivious to the fact that Frank was still shouldering his duffle bag and carrying a suitcase, Mrs. Johnson brushed past him to continue her tour of the renters' quarters. Explaining that the nearby bathroom was another shared space, she underscored her insistence that the bathroom had to remain "spic-and-span."

"I hope you're not the kind of person who leaves hair in the sink or in the shower. I won't tolerate that in my bathroom."

Frank decided on the spot to grow a beard, negating the need to shave. Glancing at his image in the bathroom mirror, he imagined what his hair might look like if it grew to shoulder length. However, he was struck by the thought that such hirsute hipness would be an immediate marker for Mrs. Johnson of a deviant troublemaker. Maybe he'd find another place before either the beard or his hair took on an appearance that would spook her. He wasn't sure whether he stood a ghost of a chance to remain in her good graces, particularly given the house rules.

"And another thing," announced the landlady. "There are no girls allowed at any time in your room. If I see or hear that you've tried to sneak a young lady up here, I'd just toss both of you out immediately."

Oh my god, an exasperated Frank sighed. There's got to be some way out of here. The sooner the better.

"And here," gesturing to the room at the end of the hall, "is your bedroom. Pretty comfy and a good deal to boot. You even have a desk, something the others don't have. I expect you'll need to unpack now. Just remember to be quiet coming and going. Here's a key to lock this room and another for the front door. Well, good night!"

"Good night, Mrs. Johnson," softly intoned a weary Frank. The combination of the long drive and the drill-sergeant routine of his landlady had drained any desire to go out. All he wanted to do was to unpack and relax a little before hitting the sack. Flopping down on the bed added one last insult to his senses as he sank into the mushiest mattress he had ever encountered.

What a contrast to the place and the person with whom Frank had spent the last several months. Instead of a small bare bedroom among strangers, he had lodging in a tidy house with a large basement, lined with bookshelves of enticing volumes. Centered equidistant from the surrounding bookshelves was a pullout bed for both sleeping when he could and reading when he couldn't. The owner of this domicile was a handsome elderly widow whose stark white hair was cropped, offsetting her soft facial features. Her equanimity and hospitality radiated outward from her Quaker demeanor, enveloping Frank in an environment that approximated a slimmed down version of a Gandhian ashram.

This restful living space, just outside the city of Naperville, Illinois, was one of the few perks that Frank received for his volunteer work as a Vietnam Summer Intern for the American Friends Service Committee (AFSC) in the summer months of 1967. He was able to indulge his political passions of speaking and organizing against the war and the draft without monetary compensation as a consequence of having saved money from the two prior summers of laboring in Jones & Laughlin steel mill in the South Side of Pittsburgh. In addition, Frank had been awarded a tuition grant for graduate school and would be acquiring a teaching assistantship for the spring quarter. So, he did not have to worry about finances during the few months of his time as an AFSC volunteer and through the fall and winter quarters of grad school.

On the other hand, while his work during the summer of 1967 was emotionally rewarding, it also was fraught with some traumatic moments that produced both physical and mental scars. Because of his total immersion in topics related to the Vietnam War, including an obsession with the number of Vietnamese being murdered by his country in so many horrific ways by heinous weapons like napalm and anti-personnel fragmentation bombs, he drove himself to insomnia for which the books in the basement he inhabited provided a modicum of relief. The other more alarming incidents were the death threats that ensued from the publicity he attracted as an antiwar speaker and draft counselor. Among those threats was a telephone caller who menacingly hissed that Frank would soon be shipped back in a railroad coal car to Pittsburgh. Another ominous warning of imminent death was a postcard with a riflescope and his name written in the middle. The signature on the postcard was that of the extremist right-wing group, the Minutemen. While no physical harm was visited upon him in Naperville, he carried some psychological wounds with him to Minneapolis.

Ensconced now in the confined space of a rickety old bedroom with lingering thoughts about the recent past, Frank wondered whether the exhaustion of the day would help lull him into a much-needed sleep. Most of his clothes were unpacked and stuffed into the creaky drawers of the ramshackle dresser in the corner of the bedroom. The remaining duffle bag contents of one pillow and one blanket were thrown on the mattress. Several different coats, from the Pitt letter jacket to a raincoat, extracted from that same duffle bag, were soon hung on the bent wire hangers in the small closet.

Frank maneuvered himself over to the heavily stained wooden desk and pulled out the chair where he had placed his backpack. Removing a notebook from his backpack, he opened it to the page that listed the names of places and people he hoped to visit tomorrow or soon thereafter. Even if he had difficulty sleeping this evening, he looked forward to having an early and potentially sumptuous breakfast at one of the local diners, Al's. After the meal and some exploration of Dinkytown, the campus, and the West Bank, the area that bordered the other side of the Mississippi River dividing the campus into east and west sections, he would call the telephone number he had been given for Daniel Whitman. He had been told that Whitman was a conscientious objector who was attempting to start a draft referral program for the Twin Cities. Given his experience from the summer with the AFSC and his own commitment to turning in his student deferment in protest of the draft, he was hoping to join with Daniel and any others who were prepared to mount a campaign to undermine, in whatever way possible, the Selective Service System.

Closing the notebook but leaving it on the desk, Frank took out the toothbrush and toothpaste lodged in one of the pockets of his backpack. He placed those next to the tattered towel that Mrs. Johnson had deposited on the dresser. Pulling together the heavily brocaded dark green curtains across the window above the desk, he closed off the depressing view of the aluminum siding of the abutting house next door. Given the absence of even a hint of nature outside the window, the dreary-looking drapes offered the illusion of a green space.

Frank slowly undressed down to his briefs and t-shirt. Grabbing the towel, toothbrush, toothpaste, and room key, Frank made a quick dash to the bathroom. Returning to his room and putting aside the slightly wet towel and toothbrush, Frank removed his dog-eared copy of *Catch-22*. Flicking off the overhead light and turning on the tiny lamp on the small bedside table, he sank into the mattress as Yossarian once more appealed to Doc Daneeka to save him from another bombing run.

Three

"A bombing," exploded Frank. "Jesus Christ! Had you told me this guy was involved in a bombing, I would have refused to drive him with me to Canada. I don't need another liability on this trip, not to mention that I could be charged as an accessory to a crime."

"Yeh, well, he's pretty desperate. He's been with me since he arrived earlier today from Wisconsin. Obviously, he doesn't want to be seen anywhere in public, especially with the news about the explosion at the Army Mathematics Research Center on the Madison campus of UW."

"Hold on," Frank interjected. "Was this guy involved with that action? I mean I realize that place was aiding the military with counterinsurgency operations in Vietnam. But blowing it up? I just hope there was no one in the building or anywhere near the place."

"The explosion was in the middle of the night and they called to warn the cops to empty out the building."

"Still, who knows what kind of repression is going to come down on lots of different folks as a consequence."

Frank's friend didn't have time to engage in a discussion about the ramifications of the bombing. He just wanted to make the transfer as quickly and quietly as possible. "It's still dark enough now and I can transfer him from my car to yours and then you can hit the road. Besides, aren't you already going to be adding another charge to your rap sheet by fleeing the states?"

Frank rubbed his forehead and pondered his predicament. He couldn't deny that he was already compounding what the state deemed as "illegal" actions from his involvement with the destruction of draft files to running away to Canada. But, really, he had tried to remain nonviolent even as his militancy and that of the movement, in general, increased. Was this flight now with a bomb-throwing passenger indicative of the erasure of the more definitive boundary between his commitment to nonviolence and a turn to revolutionary violence? Expelling a long sigh, Frank nodded to his friend. "Okay, move him into my car."

Waking up his passenger, Frank's friend took the guy's duffle bag from the backseat and threw it into the open trunk of the Corvair. He then gently pushed the stranger into the back of Frank's car where the scruffy-looking guy curled up on the floor.

"He'll probably sleep most of the way to International Falls. It might be best not to ask any questions."

Frank just shook his head in resignation. He looked at his friend for possibly the last time. Believing that he had dispelled all of his doubts about leaving the country, the pained expression on his face reflected all the lingering questions that now re-emerged, seemingly unresolved. He reached out to embrace the only person besides Mary who knew that Frank planned to disappear.

"Good luck, brother," he whispered in Frank's ear.

"Yeh, same to you," replied Frank as he let go of more than he could admit.

Four

A sharp pain startled Frank awake. He had rolled over on his copy of *Catch-22* with the remaining paperback bookbinding lodged between the upper ribs on his left side. Sitting up as best he could in the swayback mattress, he picked up the book and placed it on the nightstand next to the lit lamp. The closed curtains blocked any view of the outside. Lumbering over to the window, he drew back the drapes. Still dark. Without the benefit of either a watch or a clock, he had no way of knowing the time. This meant that he would have to trudge down the hall to the kitchen where a large wall clock hung over the oven. Once he had pulled up his well-worn jeans, he slowly opened his bedroom door.

Trying to be as quiet as possible, he tiptoed along the uneven boards of the wooden floor. He passed a closed door of another renter and then the open bathroom before reaching the kitchen. There was not even a hint of light shining into that area through the large window that looked out onto the backyard. Feeling along the wall for a switch, Frank flicked on an overhead florescent light. As it sputtered on, he could see that the two hands on the clock were pointing downward together. So, if this was the correct time, it was 5:30 A.M.

"Damn," Frank uttered under his breath. He couldn't believe that he had been able to sleep for seven hours straight. It had been several months since he had any significant uninterrupted rest. Maybe this was a sign that his insomnia was just a phase tied to the intense summer activities. Although still very early, he saw no need to go back to bed. Instead, remembering that Al's Diner opened at 5 A.M., he returned to his room to retrieve his towel for the morning ablutions. Not wanting to risk taking a shower this early in the morning, he quickly washed his face and smoothed down his slightly unruly hair.

Once back in the bedroom, he put on a short-sleeved shirt and stuffed a sweatshirt into his backpack along with the notebook. Surveying the room for anything else he might need to take with him, Frank made sure that his wallet was still lodged in the very bottom of the backpack. He knew he had at least one hundred dollars in cash, enough for several meals out, buying food for the rest of the week, and a few of the books needed for his classes. He would need to set up a checking account soon and transfer money into it from savings back in Pittsburgh. For now, however, he was ready to head out into the early morning pre-dawn streets of Dinkytown.

Wending his way over to 14th Avenue, Frank turned in the direction of Al's. Against the darkness surrounding the other stores, the diner's lights illuminated the pavement outside, beckoning anyone in this early hour to come inside. Eager to accept this glowing invitation to enter, Frank pulled open the glass door and wedged himself into the line that had formed behind the seated diners. How in the hell, he wondered, did the place already have a group of people standing in anticipation of procuring one of the coveted seats? It looked like there were only a dozen or so stools, all occupied, with maybe half that number waiting to wrest the first vacated seat.

It seemed to Frank that all those seated were young and middle-aged men chowing down before their workday would begin. Standing behind two grizzled older guys in such close proximity, he could not avoid overhearing their animated conversation.

"So, Sam, I gotta tell ya, I'm thinking that the Twins got a real shot this year for the American League pennant. What with Killabrew swatting homers and Carew and Tony O peppering the outfield with hits, they are going to give the Red Sox and White Sox a run for the money."

"Hey," Sam replied, "don't forget the Tigers. I mean those teams are all evenly matched and bunched up at this point."

"Wait, are the Tigers still able to play in their home field? Didn't it get burned to the ground in that riot last month?"

"No way, you think the Army and tanks were brought in to just tame the natives? Naw, they had to protect Tiger stadium. Anyhow, I just wish some of them colored snipers would have picked off McClain and Lolich. It would have made it easier for us in the remaining games we have with them."

It took Frank some effort not to interject his pointed responses to this overheard conversation. He would, of course, have told them that it was no riot, but a righteous rebellion. And there were no snipers picking off white folks. In fact, the trigger-happy white National Guard murdered scores of Blacks in cold blood. Before he could blurt out his political "corrections," the two had changed the subject to another sport.

"I just wish the Vikings hadn't traded away Tarkenton. Who knows what this guy Kapp is gonna do. And who's this new coach, Graham or something like that?

"I think his name is Grant, Bud Grant."

"Well, at least there are those big guys on defense, Page and Eller."

Chomping down on his last piece of bacon from the plate, Sam shook his head as if to acknowledge that the Vikings defensive front line certainly put the hurt on every team they played. Then, both guys got up almost simultaneously from their seats. Plunking down some bills and coins, they shouted in unison, "See ya later, Al."

Squeezing by Frank, they exited the diner along with a few other customers. In the process, those standing, including Frank, immediately swiveled onto the empty stools. While the others called out their orders, he searched for a menu. Not finding anything that resembled a list of breakfast items, he addressed the waitress who stood patiently in front of him: "Do you do poached eggs?"

"Does this look like some fancy restaurant? We gotta grill for either scrambled, fried, or once over easy. Take your pick."

"I'll go with the scrambled and sausage. Does toast come with that?

"Sure does. You want coffee?

"Yeh and a glass of water would be great."

Within a few minutes, Frank's order appeared all stuffed on a large plate. Jammed into one corner of the plate was an ample portion of home fries. Without stopping to inquire about ketchup, he began shoveling the food into his mouth. As more customers started coming through the door, Frank hurried along with his meal. Out of hunger and a desire to get some breathing room, he scarfed up every little morsel. The bill, tucked underneath the plate, was easily covered by the loose bills he had in his pocket, leaving a generous tip to boot.

By the time Frank exited Al's Diner, the sun had begun to peek over a few wispy clouds, providing enough daylight to survey the surroundings. Perine's, the nearby large book repository, was still closed. Besides, Frank had heard about another more idiosyncratic bookstore on the West Bank that he planned to visit after traversing the campus. He could see the university just on the other side of University Ave. He intended to get the feel of the campus without the crush of students who would soon begin the new term.

Walking towards University Ave., Frank once again noticed the iron bridge that seemed an appropriate symbol of the transition to and from Dinkytown. This time as he sauntered over the bridge, he noticed the words "Frodo Lives" in large painted white letters. Bemused, he wondered who this person might be. It certainly wasn't any third world revolutionary known to him. Maybe the bookstore owner on the West Bank would be able to unlock the mystery of who Frodo was and why the reference to his sentient existence.

Crossing University Avenue, Frank entered the clearly designated campus of the University of Minnesota. Myriad verdant trees punctuated the grounds, offsetting both permanent and temporary-looking structures. In fact, a sign identified one of those less permanent buildings as "Temporary North of Mines." For a brief moment, he entertained the idea of committing a prank by changing just one letter on that sign so it would read "Minds" instead of

"Mines." Then, maybe the space inside could be used for a philosophy course on epistemology or an abnormal psychology class.

Navigating through the maze of walkways, Frank soon emerged onto a square bordered by stately structures that he would later learn was called "Northrop Mall." At the north and south ends were two buildings that proudly advertised themselves as imitations of Greek architecture. Several of those edifices would become sites for protest and occupations in the next few years. For now, they all seemed, with the exception of Coffman Union, the student center that sat across Washington Ave., to be rather off-putting. Indeed, Frank did not see the need to tarry to take in the architectural symmetry of the buildings or to explore the offices and rooms inside each although searching out the library would become a critical objective soon enough.

He increased the tempo of his stride, moving briskly toward the Washington Ave. Bridge. As he stepped onto the pathway, he stopped momentarily to admire the beauty of the Mississippi River as it flowed below. In the future when Frank no longer wished to view any river in the United States, including the mighty Mississippi, this bridge and the body of water underneath would become the tragic site for the suicide on June 7, 1972 of the poet and University of Minnesota professor, John Berryman. There was a double irony, therefore, as the lanky young Frank fell into a poetic reverie about the power and majesty of this river.

After the brief interlude, he continued his trip across the bridge. Passing through an area with newer and more sterile-looking structures, Frank made his way into the West Bank. He soon located the old firehouse that had become the residence of Martin McGosh and his massive collection of books. The large front door appeared open. So, without any hesitancy, Frank walked in and was immediately accosted by a rather jolly looking bearded gentlemen who was either a reclusive wizard or the proprietor of this strange, but marvelous, bookstore. It was, of course, the latter although McGosh gave off a vibe of mysterious wizardry at work.

"What can I do you for, young man?"

"Are you Mr. McGosh?"

"I am, indeed, that very gentleman."

"Perhaps you can help me solve something I saw that puzzled me."

"Well, I'm no puzzle master although I have been known to enjoy a riddle or two."

"I just came from Dinkytown and..."

Before Frank could explain what captured his imagination, McGosh spit out the words, "That benighted place. You know, I used to live there and have a bookstore in a building there until they forced me out. At least, it caused a little trouble for the rascals that evicted me when students showed up to protest."

Frank contemplated the possibility that "Frodo" was, in fact, a nickname for McGosh.

"Did you ever go by the name of 'Frodo,'" he inquired.

McGosh began laughing loudly and shaking his head at the same time. Addressing the confused lanky lad standing before him, McGosh took a moment to compose himself.

"Son, I take it you've never read *The Lord of the Rings* or anything by Tolkien?"

Frank had never heard of the book or the author. In order not to appear completely ignorant, he ventured a half-hearted response, "I'm not sure."

"You're not sure," McGosh thundered. "Bah, come this way, boy."

McGosh turned on his heel with Frank dutifully following him. Snaking in and out of jammed bookshelves and piles of those that were either discarded or had not yet found a suitable filing, McGosh led him to an area labeled "Fantasy." Removing one of the numerous Tolkien titles, the elderly proprietor of the bookstore opened a page to the exact description of a character called "Frodo," a Hobbit resident of Middle Earth as Frank could see from McGosh's insistent pointing of his index finger. Snapping the book closed, the wizened bookseller handed him this copy of *The Fellowship of the Ring*.

"Take this book, son, and come back when you've finished reading it. It's on me. I think you'll find out a lot more about Frodo than contained in that abbreviated graffiti could ever reveal."

Frank was a little taken aback at having the book thrust into his hands from the bookstore owner as a generous gift.

"Oh, one final thing," McGosh offered, "Don't you dare come back here if you're going to prattle on about how I remind you of Gandalf."

Not knowing what to say, Frank accepted the gift, looked up at McGosh and just replied with a sincere "Thank you."

"Don't mention it although you obviously have. Now, I've got to attend to some business. You can stick around and peruse the books to your heart's content. Just close the damn door on the way out. I didn't intend for it to be open at this early hour since I usually don't let anyone in until later in the morning."

Frank felt obliged not only to check out the other books, but also to buy something. He began to examine a section labeled as "Philosophy." Having wanted to read some Camus, he grabbed a used copy of *The Rebel*. Running to catch up to Mr. McGosh, Frank pulled out some money that he presented to the now distracted bookseller.

"Good choice, kid. See you later." And with that McGosh disappeared into the dense forest of books while Frank walked out the front door into the bright morning sun.

Five

AUGUST 25, 1970

With the sun beginning to shine through the evergreens on the side of the highway, Frank attempted to determine if his mysterious passenger was still asleep. Already one hour north of Minneapolis and headed to the border crossing at International Falls, his curiosity about who was on the floor was gnawing away at him. There hadn't been even a peep out of the guy.

In his haste to leave, Frank had forgotten to piss. Now, all that coffee he had consumed earlier was pushing propulsively at his bladder. He was going to have to pull over soon to take a pee, preferably in a wooded section of the highway. To do that, however, would also mean probably waking up the guy. Hopefully, the stranger would rouse himself soon.

As Frank tried to triangulate how far he could drive with pressure building on his bladder while seeking a remote roadside spot, he heard some rustling from behind. A loud yawn and then movement indicated his passenger had finally awakened. Glancing in the rear view mirror, he could see the wisp of a moustache on a drawn face.

"Where are we and who are you?" came the voice from the backseat.

"We are about an hour and a half north of Minneapolis with maybe three more hours ahead of us until we reach the Canadian border. I'll be crossing over and then turning east to Toronto."

"Good. I've got a contact there. Now, what did you say your name was?"

Frank realized that it would not make any sense for him to divulge his real name just as he would not expect his passenger to provide his identity. Thus, he responded somewhat nonchalantly, "Let's just call each other comrade for now."

"Fine with me. However, I assume you've got a driver's license so you can get across the border. I've got a fake ID if the pigs ask for any identification."

"I think we'll need some sort of rationale for why we're going to Canada. How's saying we're meeting some friends to go fishing on Rainy Lake?"

"Sounds like you know this area well enough for something like that to get us over the border."

"Yeh, well, I'm just wondering if there'll be any alerts out because of what happened in Madison."

Peering now through his glasses and sticking his face next to Frank's, the stranger whispered slowly in Frank's ear, "We know nothing..."

"Understood. Would you mind if I pull over soon to take a leak?"

"Be my guest. I'm holding it until we get safely over the border."

Noticing a clearing at the side of the road empty of any cars or trucks, Frank slowed down the Corvair. The car jerked to a stop. The passenger submerged himself, hidden out of view. Frank pushed open the door and exited, looking for a suitable site to relieve himself in the copse of trees nearby.

Six

AUGUST 31, 1967

Once he was outside, Frank surveyed both sides of the street. Having located the sought after public telephone booth, he headed in that direction. Once he reached the booth, he checked his pockets for any coins. Shouldering his way inside, he slid his hand into his backpack pocket to retrieve the piece of paper containing Daniel Whitman's telephone number. He hoped Whitman would answer.

After a few rings, a laconic voice softly intoned: "Dan here. Who's calling?"

"Hey," Frank started to respond rather hesitantly, "Um, you don't know me, but I got your name from the Center for Conscientious Objectors."

The voice now sounded more commanding. "So, you want to apply to be a CO?"

"No," Frank immediately replied, "I just got to Minneapolis to start grad school and am planning to turn in my draft card. I want to know if you and any others will be organizing for the national turn-in in October?"

There was an initial moment of silence and some muffled voices in the background. When Dan Whitman spoke once again, he gave Frank an address and told him to show up as soon as he could.

The street number given to him was not that far away. It didn't take long for Frank to navigate the maze of West Bank homes and apartment buildings to locate the address. Approaching the two-story wooden house, he excitedly knocked on the weather-beaten front door. When the door swung open, there stood one of the whitest persons Frank had ever seen. Straggly blond hair and wisps of blond whiskers accentuated the whiteness. Smiling ever so slightly, Dan Whitman extended his hand.

"Are you the guy who just called? Ya know, you didn't even bother to give me your name. And you are?"

"Yeh, I'm the guy. Frank Goodman is my name. Thanks so much for inviting me over."

"Sure. Any draft resister is a brother of mine. I've just got to get a few more things from my room upstairs. You can come up. And then we can go meet up with a few others at what might be the office that we're hoping to open up soon."

Dan bounded up the stairs with Frank in tow and darted into a small room with a mattress on the floor, a few brick-and-board bookshelves, and a table and a chair. On top of balled-up covers was a copy of James Joyce's *Finnegan's Wake.*

Pointing to the book, Frank queried Dan, "You have any idea what Joyce is on about in that book. I had a hard enough time getting through *A Portrait of the Artist as a Young Man* in one of my undergrad English courses at Pitt. That whole description of hell scared the crap out of me and I'm not even Catholic."

Dan looked at Frank and then to the book lying on the bed. "You know, I heard you need to have the book mounted on something like a Buddhist prayer wheel to best understand the symmetrical quality of the beginning and ending. I'll give it to you when I finish although I'm not sure when that will be."

Frank thanked him for the offer, but begged off with the excuse that he would soon be buried in all kinds of reading for his grad classes.

"You really think that getting more of a mis-education in our esteemed (here Dan hissed this word as if it were a broken hot water heater) institutions of higher learning is a substitute for an autonomous education? We need to topple those establishment ivory-covered towers that do little more than reinforce the status quo."

Frank was not sure about how to respond to this critical blast from an ostensible comrade. He soon would come to recognize that Dan's unremitting antagonism to any and every institution of the hated system was a fixed ideological position from which Dan would never swerve. So, Frank kept quiet and hoped that his nodding head would convey some level of assent to what Dan said.

"Hey, ho, let's go! It's just a short distance, but I suspect it will be a long meeting. You got any food with you?"

"I just ate an enormous breakfast. I think I still have a banana and apple in my backpack. So, I'm alright for now."

Calling out to no one in particular in this collective household, Dan yelled that he was leaving and wouldn't be back until later in the day. A disembodied loud grunt came from somewhere on the second floor.

"Must be Larry. I should have realized that he might be trying to rest before his afternoon shift begins."

Following behind Dan, Frank mimicked his slow-paced and hushed descent down the stairs and out the front door. Once outside, Dan shifted gears in his ambulatory speed. He also began pointing out some of the stores we passed.

"If you ever need any used furniture, there's a Salvation Army not far. Most of us go to "Dirty Don's" since he seems to have the cheapest prices around even if the quality is not up to the "high" standards of the Salvation Army."

With Dan as a tour guide to the Cedar Riverside shops, Frank began to get a feel for this neighborhood adjacent to the west bank of the Mississippi River. Everything from funky bars to fusty stores. In a short while, Dan stopped at a three-story brick building. He opened the front door and motioned Frank towards the steps leading to the second and third floors.

"Go up to the third floor," he called out.

As they arrived on that level, a short dark apparition approached them. Squinting at Dan, he launched an ominous scowl in Frank's direction and gruffly asked, "Who's this guy?"

Before Dan could answer, Frank held out two fingers in a peace sign and exclaimed, "Another draft resister."

Apparently, this didn't placate the grumpy interlocutor. Dan then explained what little he knew about Frank, hoping that it would put the guarded character at ease. It helped, but it also took a little time before this slightly rotund person finally would offer his hand for a shake. When he did, it was accompanied by an almost stentorian announcement of his name.

"I'm Jim Penny. No need to joke about that last name. I got baited and bullied enough about my name and my size as I was growing up."

Trying to ingratiate himself, Frank wondered if Jim was from somewhere around here. He responded that he was from a part of northern Minnesota called the Iron Range. Most of his family had worked the mines there for generations, extracting iron ore. He began to get more animated as he talked about some of his radical ancestors who had joined the Industrial Workers of the World, mentioning a great uncle who had protested the U.S. entrance into World War I and then crossed the border into Canada to escape the draft.

"Wow, that's a great legacy," enthused a truly impressed Frank.

"Yeh, well, I guess my dad forgot about that. Maybe it's because he's an insurance salesman. Anyhow, he's such a super-patriot that he has denounced me for my anti-war activities. I'm sure once he finds out that I am going to renounce my CO status, something that already pissed him off, and protest and refuse the draft, he'll bar me from ever returning home."

This last comment sent up a red flag in Frank's consciousness. He had yet to tell his parents of his decision to turn in his student deferment and risk going to prison for draft resistance. He hoped they would understand, or, at least, not disown him.

Dan broke the glum silence with an upbeat pronouncement, "Hey, we've got work to do here. Let's not stand around, paralyzed by morbid thoughts. John and Fred should be coming soon. We can start thinking about an agenda."

All three entered a mostly barren open space. There was a large desk in one corner with an old Remington typewriter on top, a four-drawer metal cabinet, and one wooden bookshelf, the latter already filled with a variety of books from manuals about the Selective Service system and draft counseling to Herbert Marcuse's *One-Dimensional Man,* the latter something Frank had heard about and was looking forward to read.

Once again, Dan assumed the task of identifying a number of agenda items for the meeting: 1.) office supplies; 2.) funding; 3.) producing leaflets; 4.) speaking engagements; and 5.) demonstrations. This all seemed a little overwhelming to Frank. So, he decided he would have to listen carefully and take notes in order to get up to speed.

"Oh, yeh," Dan added. "We need to nail down the name. I'm still in favor of the Twin Cities Draft Action Center."

Jim scrunched up his face. "Do you think our church sponsors will have a problem with the 'Action' part?"

"I'm sure the Quakers will accept this, along with many of our other sponsors."

Jim reluctantly raised another possible objection. "I'm wondering how this might come off in the media."

"Fuck the media," exclaimed Dan. "We can be our own media once we get the mimeograph machine back from the repair shop."

Just at that moment, John Rider appeared in the door with a box under his arm. "Did someone say mimeograph machine? Well, I've got that sucker ready to roll as soon as I take it out of the box."

Frank had a little difficulty understanding how this all-American, well-built stud fit into what he imagined to be the fellowship of draft resisters who he believed were physical and intellectual outliers. When the thin blonde Whitman and short dark Penny bounded over to embrace the obviously athletic Rider, Frank's momentary disbelief was dispelled.

John shrugged off the hugging and walked over to the desk where he deposited the box. Looking directly in Frank's direction, he asked with a frown, "Do I know you?'

"Not yet, but I hope soon. I'm here for grad school, but also intend to send my draft card back as part of the October 16 protest."

"Sounds good to me. I'm not quite there yet, especially since I want to bring along my parents for support. In the meantime, I plan on helping out in whatever ways I can. I think I've made a good start by first procuring this mimeograph machine and then getting it repaired so it can produce all the leaflets that you brainiacs will be creating."

This must have been a cue for the appearance of Fred Adamson who was excitedly waving a copy of the radical magazine, *Ramparts*. Without bothering to acknowledge anybody now in the room, Fred breathlessly read out loud specific excerpts from the Selective Service document called "Channeling" that *Ramparts* reprinted:

"'Many young men would not have pursued a higher education if there had not been a program of student deferment...Throughout his career as a student, the pressure – the threat of loss of deferment – continues.'"

Here, he paused to emphasize how these lines would be especially important to include in a leaflet for college and even high school students.

"But here's the real clincher," Fred intoned, "'The psychology of granting wide choice under pressure to take action is the American or indirect way of achieving what is done by direction in foreign countries where choice is not permitted.'"

Wanting to emphasize that last part, Fred used an officious sounding voice to repeat, "where choice is not permitted." Bringing out a button that had a red background with a black Omega symbol on it, he made reference to what was becoming a common slogan in the draft resistance movement: "Not with my body!"

Quite an entrance for this short, slight, baby-faced young man with uncharacteristically large feet. Totally unaware of Frank, Fred addressed himself first to Dan and then to Jim and John, "I'm ready to write the leaflet, mimeo it, and take it to every campus in the Twin Cities."

"Hold your horses, Fred," interjected Dan. "We've got a whole agenda to discuss. Obviously, that's a great idea for a leaflet, but we still need to review all of the other matters. First and foremost, let's agree on our name."

Dan motioned to a closet that John entered, returning with two folding chairs on either arm. Frank held back while Fred, Dan, and Jim took one chair, unfolded it, and assembled in a small circle.

"This other chair is for you, Frank," offered John.

At this announcement, Fred raised his head from *Ramparts.* "Wait, who is this new guy?"

Once more Frank was about to introduce himself, but Dan pre-empted Frank's presentation with a curt comment, "another committed draft resister who also is a new grad student."

"Great! Finally someone who will have a legitimate reason to be on campus, not like the rest of us dropouts."

As Frank was later to learn, with the exception of John Rider, the other three had all dropped out of college, either to work full-time or part-time as an organizer. A number of church and individual donations provided a small salary for Dan and Fred, the two full timers, with Jim donating what time he had beyond his hospital janitorial job. Like Frank, John was a student at the University of Minnesota, but an undergraduate.

After arriving at an expedited consensus on the name, the Twin Cities Draft Action Center, Dan went through the other agenda items. Dispensing first with the matter of supplies, noting the closeted reams of paper for typing and mimeographing, there was an animated discussion of where to obtain another desk and typewriter. John offered to buy both that he had seen at "Dirty Don's."

"You can't keep on spending your own money for this stuff," protested Jim.

"Don't worry, I got an inheritance that I'm more than happy to use for anything that will advance our agenda."

"And speaking of advancing our agenda, let's talk about creating some flyers and where and when to distribute them."

Fred was quick to offer writing a leaflet for students that incorporated the "Channeling" references he had previously articulated. Frank tentatively offered his help with producing and disseminating the leaflet on campus.

"Thanks. I hope you can also recruit some other students to get a chapter or, at least a group, at the 'U' who can build the movement and the turnout for October 16."

"I'm willing to do that," Frank now more confidently proffered.

As the five young men exchanged thoughts on other possible flyers and where to post and distribute them, a feeling of fellowship organically emerged from their mutual commitments to the tasks at hand and the ultimate goal ahead of them. Soon, the discussion gravitated to the October 16 national draft card turn-in. Not yet familiar with either the geographical or political landscape of the Twin Cities, Frank deferred to the other four.

Dan reached inside one of the desk drawers and pulled out a piece of paper on which Frank could see the bold-faced large print announcing "October 16, 1967 Draft Card Turn-In." Reading from the smaller printed text, Dan highlighted the following as a possible first paragraph for their own, Twin Cities Draft Action Center (TCDAC) flyer:

"'On October 16, 1967, we will publicly and collectively return our draft cards to the Selective Service System in major cities throughout the country. We will clearly challenge the government's right to use our young lives for its own nefarious purposes. Our challenge will continue, and we will openly confront the Selective Service System, until the government is forced to deal with our collective action...By turning in rather than burning our draft cards, we will be proudly giving our names to the public at large, and to the powers that be.'"

When Dan finished reading this passage, Jim muttered something hardly audible about adding another S to the Selective Service System and that S would stand for "Sauron." Although Frank was sitting next to him and heard what Jim uttered, he had no idea who or what Sauron was. In a much louder and more insistent voice, Fred made some suggestions for the rest of the text while Dan pointed to the need to give some specific details about where and when the demonstration would take place. Frank's only contribution was to request some language about how this would be in the great non-violent civil disobedience tradition of Thoreau. The others agreed.

After each agreed to specific assignments, the meeting broke up. Before Frank left, he had jotted down some possible language about nonviolence and civil disobedience and given it to Dan. Thanking him for his contributions and encouraging him to come back to the official office now of the TCDAC, Dan remarked, "Let's hope October 16 will have some impact and our nonviolent actions will spark even more draft resistance and civil disobedience."

Seven

AUGUST 25, 1970

Frank headed towards a clump of trees that would shield him from being seen even if, heaven forbid, another car pulled over to where the Corvair, containing his fellow fugitive and future exile, had stopped. Before pulling down the zipper on his pants, he paused to recall his passage to this point. Thinking back to that first meeting with his comrades at the TCDAC and his own insistent input on nonviolence, he tried to fathom the transformations that had led him to breaking and entering a building to destroy draft files. Certainly, he was frustrated that the war with all of its death and destruction continued unabated, even as Nixon tried to portray his policies, including instituting a lottery for the draft at the end of 1969, as "winding down the war." It seemed that, if anything, Frank and so many of his cohorts in and out of the movement were getting even more wound up.

Finishing up relieving himself of all the piss in his system, if not all the doubts about his actions, Frank walked back to the car. He could see that his passenger was staying out of sight by scrunching down in the back seat. As soon as he opened the door to the driver's side, he asked the stranger whether he wanted to sit up front. Not only did it make sense now that they were on a fairly remote stretch of the highway, but also they would need to prepare and rehearse for any eventualities once they reached the border crossing at International Falls.

"It probably does make sense to join you up front. Maybe I can also relax a little by listening to your radio."

Frank had to disabuse him of that idea since the radio had been broken after he was pounding on top of the console to the beat of Sly and the Family Stone's "I Want to Take You Higher." Either the radio took Sly's advice and lifted the frequency into the stratosphere or the pounding had so damaged it that repair wasn't an option. Of course, it didn't matter that, even with Mary's constant reminders about fixing it, Frank refused to get someone to look at the broken radio.

"Well, I don't feel in the mood to offer any of my own renditions of songs we might both know. So, I'll just try to get a little more sleep until we're within an hour of the border crossing and can rehearse our reasons for our visit (emphasis on that word) to Canada."

Frank's comment even shocked him when it came spilling out of his mouth, "Why did you do it?"

"It? I thought 'it' was not up for discussion."

"I know. It's just I've been trying to work out in my own mind how my own actions escalated. I thought maybe sharing some of our thinking would be helpful."

"Helpful to whom? I don't think you really want me to reveal what could implicate you, do you?"

"Sorry, I just don't understand why the bombing. I get that the Army Math Research Center was part of the war machine, but there were other ways to protest nonviolently what was being done."

"Do you really know what was being done by that wretched evil Center? Did you ever see my investigative reporting in the *Daily Cardinal* about the work that they were doing there for the creation of an "Electronic Battlefield" in Vietnam so they could indiscriminately slaughter even more innocent peasants over there? Did you read about all of the nonviolent protests we had done for years, pleading with the administration at the University of Wisconsin to end all ties with the Pentagon?"

Frank had to admit that he didn't know all the background and context. Then again, he also didn't know, because it wasn't yet public, of the death of one researcher and the injury of several others who were in the building when the massive bomb of ammonium nitrate and fuel oil exploded. Undoubtedly, this not only would have complicated Frank's own reaction to the bombing, but also made him resistant to taking this guy on as a passenger.

"Look, I really don't want to talk about this anymore. If you want to discuss or debate in a more abstract way nonviolence versus violence, I would consider that. For now, can I get a little more shut-eye?"

Shaking his head up and down, as much to give assent to his passenger's request as to continuing his internal debate about this and related matters, Frank demurred.

Eight

AUGUST 31, 1967

Walking back to his room in Dinkytown after his first exhilarating meeting with the fellowship of TCDAC, Frank paid scant attention to all those sights that had earlier in the day captivated him. Even the Mississippi River could not distract him from the swift-moving currents that swirled around inside his brain. Enigmatic eddies churned his consciousness, drawing him into internal debates about civil disobedience and nonviolence. So awash in these existential torrents was Frank that he almost forgot to do the necessary grocery shopping.

Only when he stepped into Dinkytown did his mind shift gears into the more mundane considerations of what food items he wanted to purchase. Inside a small grocery store, Frank immediately took stock of what provisions would sustain him for at least the next week. Grabbing a few cans of soup assured him of a quick meal for either lunch or dinner. A large box of cereal would suffice for breakfast, along with a gallon of milk. Then, he picked out some fresh vegetables like lettuce, carrots, and tomatoes for salad and a couple of apples. Not much for cooking, Frank did throw in a pound of hamburger in the cart. The hamburger could be transformed into a meat loaf that would last for several days in the fridge. It wouldn't even require reheating as long as he could pour some ketchup over it for a sandwich. A sandwich, of course, required bread. He chose a loaf of whole wheat as a marker of something more wholesome than white bread. For making an expeditious and delicious sandwich, Frank returned to the aisle where the peanut butter and jelly dotted the shelves.

With his two bags of groceries in hand, he headed towards his temporary home as dusk began to envelop Dinkytown. When he arrived at the front door, he deposited one of the bags on the porch while fishing in his pocket for the key to the front door. Once it was opened, he retrieved the bag he had set down. He trudged up the stairs and went directly into the kitchen. Opening the fridge, Frank saw a vacant area on one of the shelves where he could deposit all the items needing refrigeration. In one of the cupboards he found an empty shelf for the cans of soup and jars of peanut butter and jelly.

Since he was too tired to begin the task of making the meat loaf and he wanted something more than a salad, Frank decided to return to downtown Dinkytown and try the Japanese restaurant he had passed earlier in the day. Not wanting to keep his backpack with him, Frank started down the hall to get to his room. Just as he passed the bathroom, one of the other renters exited his room, blocking his passage. Frank was then obliged to say something to this older looking man holding a large towel.

"Hi, I'm your new neighbor," Frank said as he extended his hand as an obvious friendly gesture.

Looking down at the proffered hand and then at Frank's face, a quizzical scowl washed over the man's puffy face. Backing up without taking the offered hand or even bestowing a greeting, he simply pointed in the direction of the bathroom. Not sure how to react, Frank thought it best to just move along and get inside his room as quickly as possible.

Once inside, Frank unburdened himself of the backpack. He took out the two books obtained at McGosh's. Eager to read *The Rebel*, he tossed it on the bed where it would either seduce or sedate him after dinner. Plunking *The Fellowship of the Ring* on a corner of the desk, Frank promised himself that he would get to the Tolkien later in the week. It was a promise he never kept.

Nine

The seduction felt more like an exercise in S&M. The lash of Camus' erudition stung. It also delivered a modicum of pleasure even at the expense of Frank's intellectual deficiencies. Camus' razor-sharp reflections on rebellion drove Frank to use the yellow magic marker set strategically on the bedside table for underlining those enticing passages on the rebel and rebellion. From the philosophical re-imagining of Descartes' "Cogito Ergo Sum" as "I rebel, therefore we exist" to the definition of the rebel's project as "altruistic individualism," *The Rebel* kept Frank enthralled for hours until the mental exhaustion depleted his will to continue reading.

Putting the book aside, Frank made a final cerebral effort to try to sort out what Camus was saying about the two different, but related, forms of rebellion: the metaphysical where the renunciation of God and religion revealed the false promise of eternal salvation; and the historical where ideological certitudes could lead to totalizing politics and murder unless there was a commitment to embracing limits. Without a sense of ethical boundaries, metaphysical and historical rebellions would degenerate into nihilism. Thus, for the rebel, politics must be an extension of ethics. Moreover, as Camus made clear: "Rebellion, though apparently negative since it creates nothing, is profoundly positive in that it reveals the part of man which must always be defended."

Craving sleep but kept awake now by wanting to share his ideas about Camus with his fellow rebels at the TCDAC, insomnia once again stalked Frank. If he could just get a few hours of rest, he would have enough energy to run over to the Center and begin the process of translating these weighty ideas into accessible leaflet language. Ready to give in to the insomnia, Frank finally fell into a fitful sleep, dreaming of armies of hideous creatures, driven by an evil force, laying waste to a foreign land and its inhabitants.

Crying out, he woke up. Drenched in sweat, Frank tried to shake off the sense of doom attached to the still vibrant images that plagued his brain. Focusing on his bedside table where the light from the lamp illuminated *The Rebel*, he shook off the terrible nightmare as the ideas gleaned from Camus displaced those horrific images. Twisting himself out of the bed, he snatched a towel and a bar of soap from the top of the dresser and made a dash to the bathroom.

Because it was late in the morning, the other two renters had already left, allowing Frank the luxury of a leisurely shower. After closing the bathroom door, he hung his shorts on the towel rack. He slid the opaque plastic shower curtain, adorned with little fish, along the length of the metal bar and entered the shower. Frank fiddled with a shower handle trying to determine how to turn on the shower and locate a temperature that was neither too hot nor too cold. As cold water dribbled from the showerhead, he adjusted the handle, managing finally to get a warm spray under which he lathered up and then rinsed. He gingerly pushed in the handle, stopping the water until only a few drops signaled his exit from the shower. After drying off, he returned to his room and dressed hastily.

Looking forward to an undisturbed breakfast, he toddled over to the kitchen. First, he grabbed a bowl from the cupboard and a spoon from a drawer where a variety of odds and ends of misshapen silverware lay in a plastic divider. Finding his cereal opened, Frank made a mental note to label it after breakfast. Once he retrieved his gallon of milk from the fridge, he poured out enough liquid to submerge the brown flakes under a white lake. His spoon dove into the lake, dredging up the cereal. He drank the last puddles of milk remaining in the bottom of the bowl. Tidying up meant washing and drying the bowl and spoon and returning the now labeled cereal and milk to their respective places. Hopefully, the attention paid to cleaning up would prevent Mrs. Johnson from finding fault with his kitchen routines and any of the other roomies from exploiting further Frank's neglect to mark his rations.

Bounding down the hall, Frank entered his bedroom. He snatched *The Rebel* from his bedside table and deposited it in his backpack. Opening up the curtains above the desk, light seemed to shimmer against the aluminum siding from the house next door. Maybe it was hot enough outside to wear the t-shirt that presently draped his skinny torso. Just in case the temperature got colder, Frank went to the closet to get his sweatshirt that he then stuffed into the backpack. Surveying the rest of the room, Frank took the notebook from the desktop. Ready to go, he opened the door and locked it behind him.

Once outside, Frank rushed through Dinkytown, avoiding even the temptation to stop and read some of the menus posted outside the restaurants dotting his path. He did, however, make a mental note to drop by one of the Italian restaurants to order a pizza for dinner later in the week. Not bothering to pay homage to the "Frodo Lives" graffiti on the 4th Street Bridge, he hurried across University Avenue and dashed through the campus. He didn't linger on the Washington Ave. Bridge as he had previously done. His purpose was to get to the TCDAC office as fast as he could with the expectation that he could type up a leaflet and then make copies of it using the mimeo machine.

When Frank arrived at the TCDAC office, Dan was already sitting at the desk and talking on the recently installed telephone. As soon as Dan put down the receiver, Frank verbally accosted him with a streak of disconnected sentences containing snippets from what he had highlighted in *The Rebel*. Peppering his nonstop monologue with whatever he could remember from his fevered reading, Frank extracted the book from his backpack

"Wait, slow down," averred Dan. "I don't have a clue about what you're saying or why."

Frank took a deep breath and then proceeded to explain the inspirational material he culled from Camus' *The Rebel*. He wanted to convince Dan that there were philosophical gems that he could extract, polish, and then engrave in a compelling flyer for joining the draft resistance movement. Although skeptical, Dan did not wish to deter Frank from writing a leaflet. However, he let Frank know that before it could be made into multiple copies for distribution, some of the other members of the TCDAC would have to read it and approve using the valuable mimeograph machine for its production.

Finding one of the folding chairs nearby, he situated himself on the other side of the desk from Dan. He placed the book on the desk and took out the notebook from his backpack. Tearing off a blank sheet of paper, Frank started writing how the rebel, in the words of Camus, "affirms the existence of a borderline" that he will not cross. Frank accused the Selective Service System of destroying that borderline by inducting young men to kill others. Addressing potential draft resisters, Frank urged them to join in a movement of rebellion and solidarity. Quoting once again from *The Rebel*, he cited this passage from Camus: "Solidarity is founded on rebellion, and rebellion, in turn, can only find its justification in this solidarity."

As he was furiously scribbling this philosophical screed on draft resistance and rebellion, Frank was unaware that Jim, Fred, and John had wandered into the office. Each apparently had a list of contacts at different colleges and high schools throughout the Twin Cities. Comparing names, they were beginning to generate a master list that would become a primary resource for the TCDAC.

After finishing his sloppily written draft, he dragged the typewriter across the desk. A box of carbon copy paper lay nearby. Inserting the carbon copy between a blank piece of white and smirched yellow paper, Frank aligned them and then scrolled the three sheets into the typewritten. He managed to fill the whole page with his verbiage. Eager to have his comrades read the completed text, he interrupted their confab and handed to Jim and Fred the two typed copies.

"Please give me your feedback so we can get some consensus on a leaflet."

When Fred finished, he wrote something on the smirched yellow paper. Jim did the same on the white paper and then handed it off to John. When John finished with his comment, he turned to the blank side of the white paper and penned some lines that he shared with the others. They nodded and John handed off to Frank the marked papers on which Jim had written, "too academic;" Fred had written "too philosophically dense;" and John had written "too many words." On the other side, in bold capital letters were the brief declarative sentences: DRAFT CARD TURN-IN. DON'T BE A SLAVE TO THE SSS OR TURNED INTO CANNON FODDER. JOIN US. OCTOBER 16. OLD FEDERAL BLDG.

Frank was incredulous and a little hurt. Fred saw the look on Frank's face and remarked, "Hey, getting out a leaflet is always a longer process with plenty of re-writes. We'll work on it over the next few days. Just drop some of the esoteric stuff and make it accessible and short."

Over the next few days, Frank showed up at the office with various renditions that went through more drafts. In between the writing, he helped move another desk into the office and set up a few more bookshelves. He asked to borrow Marcuse's *One-Dimensional Man* and started to read it both in the office and back in his bedroom. Finally, they arrived at consensus for a leaflet and began running off scores of copies on the mimeograph machine. After doing about one thousand copies, Dan announced a pot-luck celebration of the first week of the TCDAC for tomorrow.

"I don't know whether I can cook up something to share," lamented Frank.

"Don't worry. Just bring a six-pack. There will be plenty of food and lots of new people for you to meet."

Frank was relieved and happy at the same time. With classes beginning next week, he might not have as much time to devote to TCDAC matters. So, he welcomed the opportunity to relax with his draft resister buddies and encounter others, especially if there were women among them.

Ten

SEPTEMBER 2, 1967

Frank decided to drive over to Dan's place for the potluck. He hadn't driven the car since he arrived in Minneapolis and he was worried that it might not budge from its parking spot. There had been prior instances when the Corvair seemed determined to foil his best-laid plans by refusing to start unless the battery received a charge. Of course, it was absurd to attribute a will to an inanimate object and, yet, the car manifested a sort of spite for being neglected. Keeping in mind the past capriciousness of this poor-man's Chevy, Frank resorted to pronouncing an incantation as if some mumbo-jumbo could be a substitute for an electrical jolt. Nevertheless, as he approached the car, he went around to the rear where the Corvair's engine was. Waving his hands, palms down, just a few inches above the hood, he uttered, ever so softly, the magic words: "Ishy-Kabibal, Ishy-Kaboob."

Fortunately, no one witnessed this lanky lad performing a rather strange ritual although the tolerance in Dinkytown for aberrant behavior was pretty high. Completing the coaxing routine and entering the car, Frank was relieved when the engine turned over with just a few choking sounds.

He realized that driving meant taking a less direct route to where Dan resided. On the other hand, he wouldn't have to walk home late at night. He might even be fortunate enough to offer a ride to a damsel in distress although why that image had popped into Frank's mind was a little bizarre. Getting a lift in a Corvair was hardly equivalent to having a gallant knight on his slick steed rescue an endangered woman from a fire-breathing dragon.

Shaking off this fantasy, he reminded himself to stop at a liquor store in order to purchase a six-pack of beer for the party. He remembered passing one in the vicinity of McGosh's bookstore. Having navigated the car through traffic and into the West Bank area, Frank located the store with a small parking lot on the side. He was able to squeeze the Corvair into the last available spot.

Frank had no idea what kind of beer his buddies would want to drink or, even, if they drank beer at all. Maybe the heavy-set clerk standing behind the counter next to an old-fashioned cash register could suggest a particular popular brand.

"Excuse me, sir, but can you recommend a good six-pack of beer?"

Putting his thumbs between the black suspenders that held up his dirty blue overalls, the red-faced clerk eyed the youth who had just made this request.

"First, let me see your driver's license, son. Then, if you're not under age, I'll give you some suggestions."

Frank dutifully handed over his driver's license. Unfortunately, he hadn't bothered to change either his card or his plate to his Minnesota address.

"I ain't too predisposed to accepting an out-of-state license, especially from some kid from Pennsylvania who could just be trying to pawn off a fake ID for beer."

Sighing, Frank tried to explain he was new in town and about to begin grad school.

"You mean, you're starting up at the 'U'."

He recognized the common reference to the University of Minnesota and replied with a nod.

"Well, I'm going to trust you this one time that you're this fella here, Franklin Roosevelt Goodman and you were born on July 4, 1945. It does sound a little fishy with that name and all. Were your parents big fans of FDR?"

Frank hesitated. Not knowing the clerk's political predisposition, a wrong answer could lead to a refusal to sell him beer. However, before he could decide the best strategic response, the big ham-handed fellow plopped a six-pack of a beer called Leinenkugels on the counter.

"Here you go, son. This one's on me. Just get your new license soon and tell all your fellow students over there at the 'U' what a great little liquor store this is on the West Bank."

Frank was flabbergasted, but immensely grateful for this kindness. Only later when he learned that a six-pack of Leinenkugel was less than two bucks did the gesture seem more like a cheap advertising investment. In any case, having procured the beer free of charge, he could make his way and his contribution to the potluck.

When he pulled onto the street where Dan lived, it was lined with automobiles on either side. There was, however, an empty space between a Ford Falcon and an older Chevy into which Frank managed to maneuver the Corvair. Clutching the six-pack in one hand, he opened the car door and sauntered over to the house. Loud music was already emanating from inside when Frank rang the doorbell. Since no one answered, perhaps because of the noise, he took hold of the handle and pressed against the thick wooden door.

Once inside, Frank was immersed in a flow of young people in various stages of inebriation. Wondering where or even whether to deposit his six-pack, he looked around to get his bearings and to determine where the kitchen might be. Up to now, everyone he saw was a stranger. While he was trying to figure out the direction he should take, a large guy in a bright red shirt stepped right up to Frank.

"Hi, I'm Donnie Donaldson. I own this house, but the four of us who reside here act like a collective, mostly of misfits, malcontents, and all-around bad-ass mother-fuckers."

Dan had warned Frank that Donnie, a 35-year-old Minneapolis fireman, could be a little overwhelming, if not downright intimidating.

"I'm Frank. I work with Dan and the others at the TCDAC."

"Oh, yeh, he mentioned you. So, you're about to start grad school at the 'U.' That could be a royal waste of time and money."

Not sure how to respond, Frank just lifted up the six-pack and inquired where he should put it.

"Out back we've got a few coolers. Try to find some space out there. Just go straight ahead through the kitchen. On your way back, grab a plate, go into the dinning room and chow down."

As Frank made his way into the kitchen and out the back door, he passed Fred on his way to re-enter the house. They gave each other an ironic military salute. Right behind his new TCDAC comrade, he noticed a rail-thin individual apparently shadowing Fred. Before Frank could remove the beer bottles and transfer them to one of the coolers, this strange-looking person verbally accosted him.

"We would like to know who you are."

Frank wasn't quite able to fathom why the reference to "we" when there was only a "he" in front of him, or, perhaps that was assuming too much about this particular character. Before he could introduce himself, this fellow fled into the house, apparently trying to catch up with Fred.

Frank returned to stuffing one of the coolers with the beer. As he leaned down to check out the other drinks inside the cooler, he heard above him a women's voice.

"That was the querulous weirdo, Ed Golub. For some reason he always hangs around Fred."

When Frank stood up, he was looking down at a glowingly beatific face, framed by strawberry blonde hair. Peering into enticing blue eyes, he was star-struck but stammered a halting hello.

Not waiting for him to do the introductory honors, she extended her hand. "Hi, I'm Mary Browne. And you are?"

He wanted to say that he was smitten, but offered instead: "I'm Frank Goodman."

"Well, Frank, what brings you here? Not just to this potluck, but to our little part of the world. I know most folks around here since I've lived in and around the West Bank and Cedar Riverside for the last four years. So, you must be new."

"Yeh, that's right. I'm starting grad school in a few weeks in American Studies and I've been working with my fellow draft resisters in the TCDAC since I got to town a week or so ago."

"Wow, what a coincidence. I'm also beginning grad school in American Studies. I guess we'll be classmates."

Frank was hoping that he and Mary might not confine their intercourse to just an intellectual pursuit in their chosen academic program. Obviously, his suppressed id was finally awakening from its long slumber. The vivacious young women standing in front of him had lit a fire under that dormant entity. Attempting to hide the rising unleashed desire, he tried to keep the conversation focused on more mundane matters.

"So, you said you know everyone around here. How come?"

"Oh, I was an undergrad at the 'U' these last four years. And I've hung around the beats and the rebels who stand out like sore thumbs among the towheads who never bother to question where they are going or why. So, why have you become a draft resister?"

Frank didn't have a pat answer to give to that question even though he had spent over two years or so pondering what it meant to have a student deferment and how that made him a willing participant in the reprehensible war machine.

"I guess I hadn't thought about it when I first registered at eighteen. Once I became more conscious of what was going on with the war in Vietnam and the U.S. role, helped along by reading, teach-ins, and demonstrations, I switched my political commitments from civil rights to antiwar activism. Not that I ever separated from supporting my Black brothers and sisters. It's just that they seemed to want whites in the movement to work in their own communities and confront the realities of white racism. I mean I loved setting up a Freedom School in the Hill District of Pittsburgh, but I realized maybe I was coming off as some sort of missionary. Anyhow, as far as my draft status, I first considered becoming a conscientious objector and then decided that would still be too much of a compromise with the system. So, I signed the "We Won't Go" statement that circulated last year and committed myself to turning in my draft card this October."

Frank stopped to draw a breath after this breathless monologue. Mary seemed riveted but also a little bowled over by this non-stop spurt of personal revelations.

"Sorry," he said. "I didn't mean to go on this autobiographical binge. Why not tell me more about you?"

"Well, where do you want me to begin?"

"How about where you were born and when?"

"In Joplin, Missouri on January 1, 1946."

"No way. I was born in Joplin, Missouri on July 4, 1945 at St. Joseph's hospital."

"That was the same hospital I was born in. Maybe it was the only one in town. My Dad still hadn't left the army at that point."

"My Dad did and we all left there a few months after I was born to return to where all the rest of the family was in the Pittsburgh area."

"We came back here to Minneapolis and my Dad got a job with the electric utility company."

"My Dad went back to school, got a master's degree and wound up selling furniture before he opened his own store. You have any siblings?"

"Yeh, two younger brothers. One of the reasons I left home as soon as I could."

Both seemed so taken with each other and especially the amazing coincidences that they were oblivious to the light rain that had begun to fall. The misty precipitation had led all of the other outside stragglers to vacate the backyard.

"Maybe we should go in," Frank offered. "I'm actually starved since I never made it to the dining area."

Gently taking him by the hand, Mary led him through the jammed kitchen and into the dining room. On a large table were bowls with fruit salad, half-eaten trays of lasagna, and dishes containing portions of a variety of legumes. The vast spread made Frank's stomach rumble. He dished as many items as he could possibly fit on the dessert plate in the hand that Mary previously held.

"Aren't you eating anything?"

"I already ate my fill. Besides, I promised my roommate I wouldn't get back too late."

Frank tried to hide his disappointment that Mary couldn't stay any longer.

"Are you taking the introductory American Studies seminar?" he asked.

"Sure. I'm assuming you'll be there. If you have time after class maybe we could go for a bite somewhere."

"That would be great."

As Mary said her goodbyes to others on her way out, Frank couldn't take his eyes off her even as his stomach continued to growl. Hunger obviously seemed to be the more insistent provocateur for his body's needs at this particular moment. There would be other occasions, however, where Mary would be the driving force to satiate a sexual appetite now stirring elsewhere in his skinny body.

Eleven

MID-SEPTEMBER 1967

The start of classes at the University of Minnesota in mid-September 1967 marked the transition from hot humid summer days to the increasingly crisp ones in the fall. As Frank stepped onto the bucolic campus with its walkways bordered by deciduous trees whose leaves were beginning to turn to orange autumnal colors, there was a slight chill in the air. Apparently, for the vast majority of students who were part of the crush on the first day of the Fall Quarter, the air temperature was no deterrent to the wearing of lightweight clothes. For native-born Minnesotans, grown used to the viciously frigid winter season, a fifty-five degree day was still rather balmy.

In the jungles of South Vietnam, the nineteen-year-old draftees out on search-and-destroy missions sweated under the oppressive heat and humidity, not fully comprehending that they were being used as bait to lure out into the open the stealthy Viet Cong. Meanwhile, flying high above in the cool innards of U. S. B-52 bombers, cocky Air Force crews dropped tons of heavy ordnance onto South and North Vietnamese villagers. Those not obliterated by these tremendous explosions soon became the targets of U. S. jets dropping containers of newly "improved" napalm whose adhesive properties stuck to their burning flesh. A second strafing by other planes on villagers in the North and the South, rushing into the open from obliterated schools and hospitals, would often consist of anti-personnel cluster bombs that would release hundreds of bomblets designed to maim whoever survived the previous gruesome onslaught from above.

The sky above in Minneapolis was a clear blue. For Frank, what was also clear were the sharp images of napalmed Vietnamese children, images that were published in radical magazines like *Ramparts* and that clouded his consciousness and colonized his conscience in ways that compelled him to take part in a variety of antiwar activities. Although looking forward to his grad classes, especially the introductory seminar where he hoped to see Mary, he planned to post the TCDAC flyers about the October 16 draft card turn-in in various buildings, especially Coffman Memorial Union where the student center was. If he could recruit a few other budding activists into a new campus anti-draft organization, he could eventually set up a table in the Union that might help the visibility of the resistance movement.

Shifting mental gears as he entered an older brick building where his schedule listed the "Introduction to American Studies" seminar, Frank climbed a flight of stairs to the second floor and sauntered down the hallway to the designated classroom. Once he crossed through the open doorway, he noticed that a dozen or so students, arranged in a circle of desks, were already engaged in exchanging greetings and introductions. An older, grey-haired woman, wearing an ankle-length dress with a floral pattern, was jotting down notes in a tidy ledger. Frank correctly guessed that this was Professor Margaret Emerson, the chair of the American Studies program and instructor for the seminar. Nodding in her direction, he took an empty desk that was on the opposite side of the room from where the other students were seated.

When Mary entered, he tentatively waved. She took one of the adjacent desks next to him. Seated, she turned in his direction and with a wickedly winsome smile whispered, "Glad to see you, stranger."

Frank blushed a little. Since he had not asked at the potluck for her telephone number or address, he never bothered to follow up. Instead, he offered what came off as a rather lame excuse. "Sorry, I didn't try to reach out to you. I was just jammed with last minute details for the TCDAC."

Waving aside his embarrassment at this lack of initiative, Mary seductively suggested that there might be time after class for grabbing a bite to eat. "Absolutely," Frank eagerly responded, trying not to let his imagination about where his lips and tongue might roam lead to an embarrassing salivation in Mary's face.

Having arranged for their extra-curricular rendezvous, they both now turned their attention to Professor Emerson. After offering a brief overview of the history of American Studies at Minnesota and the particulars of this term's course, the soft-spoken head of the program encouraged each student to provide a brief introduction. Frank was struck by a number of his fellow students whose introductory biographical sketches would be enhanced later by their future trajectories.

Lance Lemon could not have been more of a contrast to the collection of other grad students. Blond and sunburnt beyond belief, Lance's California surfer looks belied his rigorous intellectual capacities, especially when he was high, which was most of the time. Lance was generous with his weed and speculations about the metaphysical state of the souls of friends. Aided by his voluptuous wife, Suzi, a psych major who provided Tarot card-readings to those friends, Lance was a gracious host. He dropped out before the Winter Term, returning to California, where he became one of the original, and initially illegal, entrepreneurs in the growing marijuana industry.

Jim Waffle, a native Minnesotan, lasted longer than Lance, finishing his Masters while engaged in establishing a trail-blazing folk music journal, *Little Sunday Review*. As one of the editors, Jim may have been responsible for "outing" Bob Dylan as the Minnesota born-and-bred Robert Zimmerman. Waffle would also achieve some fame as the author of valuable liner notes on a wide variety of Smithsonian folk albums.

Another folk *aficionado*, John Teton, actually played a relatively mean blues guitar. He introduced Frank to Cream's legendary album, *Disraeli Gears*. John did complete his Ph.D. and went on to have a productive career as a professor and scholar in one of the minor, but prestigious, Ivy-League colleges.

Jennifer Johnson also whizzed through the grad program, achieving her doctorate in record time. Finding a comfortable sinecure in a Southern university as the head of its American

Studies program, she became the embodiment of the one true disciple of Professor Margaret Emerson.

Susan Treadwell took a longer time to complete her Ph.D. Her husband, a grad student in Civil Engineering, abandoned her and she dropped out to work for a time as a waitress in one of the Dinkytown Italian restaurants. She then exploited that experience for an ethnographic doctoral dissertation of waitressing, entitled, *Serving Meatballs: The Food, the Customers, and the Quotidian Grind of Being a Waitress.*

All of the above never spent much time as political activists. While their sympathies were with the antiwar movement, their sentiments were more focused on their own career paths. The two American Studies grad students who became committed leftists of different stripes were Alan Himmelfarb and Bryce Rasher. Himmelfarb, a slight, unintimidating middle-class Jew, joined a faction of the student New Left that tried to posture as working class toughs, showing up once at a meeting of antiwar activists with chains wrapped around his paunchy stomach. Himmelfarb dropped out. Rasher also dropped out, letting his paranoia, induced by equal amounts of the tumult of the times and the potent psychedelics he ingested, drive him out of the academy and into the world of the counter-cultural underground.

Unlike his erstwhile comrades in the struggle, Frank did complete his M. A. in five successive terms. By then he and Mary, who would go on to write the first feminist study of Hawthorne's women characters for her doctoral dissertation, would be legally bound. That binding and unbinding will be the substance of other chapters, but not before noting that Frank and Mary had a delightful dinner at a West Bank bar after that first seminar. From there, with alcohol fueling their already high-octane libidos, they went to Mary's and made love. Because this was his first time having sexual intercourse, Frank was so blissed out and discombobulated that it took him several minutes before he realized that the candles Mary had lit by her bed did not have switches for turning off and on. However, Frank did remain turned on for the rest of the evening and until the early hours of the next day.

Twelve

For the next month, Frank indulged his passions. From the intellectual passion engendered by his grad courses during the day to the sexual passion enlivened by Mary during frequent evening trysts, he felt ablaze with purpose. At the same time, he could not shake the periodic eruption of guilt over the privileges he enjoyed as a white, male, middle class student that afforded him these indulgences. Hence, he expanded his political passion by attending daytime and nighttime planning meetings with TCDAC and antiwar and anti-draft organizations on campus.

The specific focus for these preparations was to build support for the October 16 draft card turn-in and the October 21 March on the Pentagon. The plans for the Pentagon demonstration emerged in late August from the coalition of groups that operated under the name of the National Mobilization Committee or MOBE, as it was more often called. Because many of the organizations in the MOBE came with their own agenda for the strategy and tactics for the

Pentagon protest, there were competing visions not only for the march but also for what would happen the day before and the day after October 21. The old left parties and old line peace organizations were afraid that the youthful militant slogan of "Confronting the Warmakers" with its emphasis on civil disobedience and disruption would scare away middle class support and alienate Congressional allies. On the other hand, the new left and counter-cultural forces embraced the confrontational mood. For the emerging hippie sensibility, that confrontation was about "levitating" the Pentagon and exorcising the demons with music, dance and playful chants. For those youth who were schooled in the hard line chanting of "Ho, Ho, Ho Chi Minh, NLF is Gonna Win!" they much preferred an actual battering down of the Pentagon rather than its magical mystical levitation.

According to Dave Dellinger, one of the leaders of the MOBE who attempted to keep the disparate forces from tearing each other apart, the Pentagon demonstration would bring together the "mighty waters of many streams." Dellinger's metaphor of choice for navigating any and all of the differences within the MOBE could not adequately account for the vortex that emerged on October 21, a vortex in which Frank almost drowned.

In the dramatic days leading up to the week of October 16, Frank sensed that he was being tossed in the "mighty waters of many streams." Acting as a campus representative of TCDAC, he traveled to large universities like Mankato State in southern Minnesota to smaller colleges like Hamline and St. Johns in and around the Twin Cities. He gave talks and participated in debates sponsored by a variety of peace groups. Fortunately, the Corvair proved uncharacteristically reliable for the driving demands imposed by Frank's circuit-riding travel schedule. For those days spent at the 'U,' he worked in helping to set up a new organization, Students Against Selective Service (SASS), often staffing the table before or after his on-campus classes.

Among his comrades at SASS were two students, one grad and one undergrad, who would become stalwart activists in the student anti-war movement. Dale Coffee, the grad student, had made an unlikely journey from preparing for work in the Foreign Service to the less establishment field of Public Affairs. When he realized that his security clearance for work in the U. S. Embassy in Guatemala would mean funneling money to the large coffee plantation owners who backed the government repression and murder of indigenous insurgents and labor organizers, he withdrew his name from consideration lest that last name be drenched in the blood of Guatemalan peasants. His calm temperament was in contrast to Rudy Schreier, the undergrad dynamo whose increasingly Marxist diatribe against "bourgeois liberals" was scaring away potential SASS recruits.

Mary would also join Frank in the Coffman Union to distribute anti-draft and antiwar literature. Her presence helped to attract male students who were more taken with her looks than the leaflets she disseminated. At times this led Frank to twinges of jealousy, especially when some of those men exhibited the kind of leering behavior that bordered on physical harassment. Although Mary was more than capable of handling herself, Frank, on occasions, felt compelled to intervene. Later, alone with Mary, she would reprimand him for that intervention, which she believed was a result of his patriarchal tendencies. He would dutifully apologize as much to placate her righteous feminist anger as to smooth over any tension that might contribute to impeding their sexual recreation.

Finding the right time and place for those sexual encounters took some planning, especially given the prohibition against women in Frank's rooming house and the confined space of the tiny West Bank house that Mary shared with her roommate, Betty. More often than not, spontaneity was sacrificed in favor of scheduling the most propitious time for making love unencumbered by all the other factors that ate into their shared intimacy. Once, when they decided to get a meal at the Japanese restaurant in Dinkytown, Frank couldn't resist the temptation to bring Mary to his rooming house. Dragging Mary in tow, they both crept up to his bedroom, hoping not to arouse Mrs. Johnson during their mutual arousal. However, a few days after, Mrs. Johnson let him know that he would have to vacate no later than November 1. Without providing an explanation for his expulsion, Frank understood that she probably overheard the muffled sounds from above and assumed, rightly, that he had transgressed the rule against having women over. When he informed Mary of his upcoming expulsion, she immediately located another roommate for the accommodating Betty in a nearby West Bank abode. Once Betty moved out, Frank transported his meager belongings across the Mississippi River and into the pleasures and eventual pain of cohabitation.

Before the move, he was so preoccupied with the demands of the October demonstrations, both planned and unplanned, that there was actually very little intimate time spent with Mary. While she was supportive of all of his activist efforts, the ever-studious Mary exempted herself from all of the events during the hectic week of October 16-21.

Indeed, the October 16 draft resistance demonstration in Minneapolis at the Old Federal Building on 3rd and Washington was an all-male affair. There were, of course, women, like Jim Penny's sister Eileen, who were prominent participants in the activities of the TCDAC. On the other hand, the two dozen protestors who showed up for the 8:30 A.M. draft card turn-in on October 16 in downtown Minneapolis were exclusively young men of draft age. Of these a dozen or so were prepared to hand over their draft cards and declare their opposition to keeping their student deferment. When Frank and four others were denied access by U. S. Federal Marshals to the building housing the Selective Service Office, a half dozen draft cards were dropped at the feet of one of the marshals.

Before leaving, Frank addressed the gathered draft resisters with the following excerpt from the letter he had previously sent to his Selective Service Board back in Pittsburgh:

Enclosed you will find my Selective Service Registration Certificate and Notice of Classification. I have returned these two items to you as an attestation of my irrevocable disaffiliation from conscription and as a protest against the Vietnam War. I realize the consequences of such action (five years in prison and/or ten thousand dollar fine), but I can no longer cooperate with a dehumanizing system that provides the unleashing of mass impersonal violence as a solution to the perceived "national interest."

In the present circumstances conscription is not only an unjustifiable infringement upon the conscience of the individual, but also it reduces the registrant to subservient collusion with the dictates of the warfare state. The new draft law is particularly reprehensible because of the inequitable deferments. Any male attending college and maintaining normal progress towards a degree is deferred. Those who cannot afford to go to college supply the overwhelming amount of the cannon fodder for the war machine of a government in which most have no real political voice. Therefore, we see that over 20% of the U. S. combat deaths in Vietnam are Negro even though they represent only 11% of the total population in the United States. Certainly, this inequity should have no place in a true democracy. To comply with conscription, then, is to sanction the imposition of militaristic "values" upon reluctant young inductees and to legitimize captive classifications for the others.

Furthermore, the draft is now providing the manpower to prosecute an illegal and immoral war. This country has no justification to send its military forces anywhere in the world to protect tyrants. We have done this in Vietnam. Instead of letting the Vietnamese decide their own future, we have intervened in a civil war at the insistence of the avaricious military-industrial-political complex in this country. We are engaged in a war in which we are murdering innocent people with weapons and methods that annihilate whole villages.

I cannot accede to a system that dictates to, discriminates against, and destroys the will of the people both here and abroad; therefore, I must sever all connections with conscription.

The scattered applause and cheers from the small gathering buoyed Frank's disappointment at the turnout and lack of dramatic confrontation that he and his comrades at the TCDAC expected. Later, he learned about the more volatile and well-attended actions that occurred on Monday in Oakland, California and into the following week. At 5 A.M. on October 16, over 200 people blocked the entrance to the induction center in that city. In the spirit of nonviolent civil disobedience, all accepted arrest. However, the next day, as several thousand demonstrators marched on the Oakland Induction Center, police clashed with protestors, especially beating the heads of those without any protective gear. The resultant bloodletting, punctuated by cries of police brutality, may have exhausted the urge for confrontation. The next day's action at the Induction Center consisted of picketing by nearly five hundred with one-fifth committing nonviolent civil disobedience and getting arrested in the process. However, by Friday October 20, the militant baton handed off to the "Stop the Draft Week" participants resulted in a massive outpouring of ten thousand demonstrators, many engaging in street tactics that maximized disruption and minimized injuries as part of running battles with the cops.

In cities around the country from New York to Chicago to Seattle, that week saw efforts to block induction centers, resist the draft, and confront any representatives of the war effort. At the University of Wisconsin in Madison the protest against Dow Chemical recruiters on campus was met with police violence. The response to the police provocation against protesting students created a lingering sense of militant anger against any and all remnants of collusion with the war machine on the Wisconsin campus, targeting, in particular, the Army Math Research Center.

Meanwhile, as part of the plans for the October 21 March on the Pentagon, almost one thousand draft cards were delivered to the Department of Justice in Washington, DC on Friday, October 20, by a prominent group of professors (Noam Chomsky, R. W. B. Lewis), clergy (Rev. William Sloane Coffin), writers (Denise Levertov, Robert Lowell, Dwight MacDonald, and Norman Mailer), and others (Dr. Benjamin Spock) on Friday afternoon. As a consequence of their support for draft resistance, a number of these eminent individuals would be indicted for aiding and abetting the violation of the Selective Service Act. Their statement that accompanied the action of the day made clear their intent to break the law. It read, in part: "The draft law demands that we shall not aid, abet or counsel men to refuse the draft. But as a group of clergy have recently said, when young men refuse to allow their conscience to be violated by an unjust law and a criminal war, it is necessary for their elders, their teachers, ministers, and friends to make clear their commitment in conscience and *aid, abet and counsel* them against conscription."

As the events were unfolding in D. C. and Oakland on that Friday, three buses left Minneapolis for the long drive to Washington. One of the passengers was Frank Goodman. For the second time in 1967, he eagerly anticipated joining the throngs of people drawn to a national antiwar demonstration on the East Coast. In mid-April, Frank and one of his closest friends had hitched a ride with a University of Pittsburgh professor to New York City where they had arranged to meet up with another friend outside of one of the hotels adjacent to Central Park, the assembly point for the march to the United Nations. As historic as that demonstration was in its massive number of participants, roughly half a million, and speeches, among the most fervent being Martin Luther King, Jr. in his new and controversial role as an outspoken opponent to the Vietnam War, Frank counted certain quirky moments as even more memorable. From encountering an old man who claimed to have been in the 1905 Bloody Sunday demonstration against the Russian Czar to following a giant papier-mâché Yellow Submarine into Sheep's Meadow in Central Park and witnessing the exhilarating burning of draft cards, he was mesmerized by those others recounting or enacting passages of rebellion.

Now, traveling on one of the Minnesota buses headed for Washington, D. C. "March on the Pentagon," he excitedly expected to become, as Camus would say, a "man in revolt." Just what kind of rebellious acts would unfold were beyond his comprehension as he reflected on his past and projected into his future. Periodically nodding off to sleep, especially in the darkness that enveloped the bus as it drove along mid-western highways, he woke up with a start to observe the morning sun beginning to rise over the familiar hilly terrain of his western Pennsylvania home.

Thirteen

AUGUST 25, 1970

His passenger, asleep for the last two hours, suddenly awoke only about one hour from International Falls and the crossing into Canada. Shading his eyes against the glare of the mid-morning sun, the mysterious stranger gazed at the driver.

"Where are we?"

Frank motioned in the direction of all the firs lining the road and responded: "We're near the Kabetogame State Forest, close to all the lakes that make up the watery entrance to Voyagers National Park."

"Ok. Thanks for the tour guide, but how far are we from the Canadian border?"

"Less than an hour. I was going to wake you up a little while ago when we drove through Hibbing, Minnesota, the former home of Bob Dylan."

"Fuck Bob Dylan. He's become an apolitical country-and-western crooner without a semblance of connection to the movement. The last significant song, "Subterranean Homesick Blues" from the *Bringing It All Back Home* album, at least had politically righteous lyrics. I guess that's why Weatherman used the line from that tune to announce their political agenda: "You don't need a weather man/To know the way the wind blows." My preference would have been to embrace the last line, "The pump don't work/'Cause the vandals took the handles," and call ourselves the "Vengeful Vandals." That would have put the war-makers on notice that we were going to vandalize all the levers that kept the war machine operating."

Frank didn't really disagree with that last bit. On the other hand, as a Dylan fan, he took umbrage at his passenger's ferocious denunciation of Dylan's recent sound and direction. He preferred the tenor crooning on recent albums to the croaking voice on the earlier ones. In fact, he had purchased *Nashville Skyline* to give Mary as a gift, hoping that she would appreciate his favorite song from that record, "Lay, Lady, Lay." Not only did she find Frank's preference for that tune somewhat sexist, but also she reprimanded him for believing that the so-called gift was something she really wanted. This rebuke, of course, initiated another in the on-going argument about his selfishness and inability to understand fully her needs and wishes. Maybe his flight to Canada was really another reflection of his self-absorption.

Trying not to dwell on these thoughts, Frank re-directed his attention to reconsidering what story they would tell the customs agent on the Canadian side at the Fort Frances stop. Although the Prime Minister of Canada, Pierre Trudeau, announced that his country should be "a refuge from militarism," Frank wasn't convinced this applied to him, as a fleeing felon who destroyed draft files, and his passenger, a member of the gang that blew up the Army Math Research

Center on the University of Wisconsin campus. Not even the May 1969 pronouncement by the Minister of Manpower and Immigration, Allan MacEachen, to open the border to deserters would cover the two of them. Added to this uncertainty, one had to assume that the RCMP wouldn't give a rat's ass for either of these statements and one of those Canadian Mounties would regard Frank and his passenger as potential subversives. Or, perhaps, the individual border guard might demand to see their draft cards. Frank had ripped up his recently issued 4-F classification at the mock graduation ceremonies in mid-May 1970, declaring in front of the thousands gathered together at the University of Minnesota auditorium that he wanted to remain free of that hated symbol of enslavement to the Selective Service System.

Turning to his passenger, Frank furtively inquired, "You don't happen to have a draft card on you?"

"Are you kidding? I burned my draft card at one of the demonstrations in Madison. The fake ID I have is a Wisconsin driver's license. You don't think the Canadian authorities are going to want to see our draft cards, do you?"

Frank wasn't sure. He certainly was worried about it. But, for purposes of keeping this guy next to him calm, he answered, "Nah. I think we'll be ok, especially if we say we're going to meet some Canadian friends who have a cabin near Rainey Lake for fishing."

"You don't think that sounds a little smelly, like some dead Walleye that's been lying around in your car?"

"I don't know. You got any suggestions other than our fishy story?"

"Guess not. We'll have to hope the Canadian customs guy is not too nosy."

"Well, if we manage to get across without any hassle, we'll head right for Thunder Bay and stop to eat and fuel up before the eight-hour drive from there to Toronto. Do you have an address for where I'll drop you off?"

"I'll check when we stop, but I think it's around the University of Toronto."

"Great, that's where I'm headed. We should arrive shortly after midnight."

Hoping that there would be no hassle at the border and the Corvair would hold together for the rest of the trip, Frank settled into a wary sense of expectancy.

Fourteen

OCTOBER 21, 1967

Not sure what to expect when he arrived at the Pentagon on Saturday, October 21, Frank contemplated what he had read about the government's preparations as the bus neared completion of the Pennsylvania Turnpike leg of the journey to Washington, D.C. According to the newspaper reports, the tens of thousands of demonstrators would be met by 1500 Metropolitan Police, 2500 National Guard, 200 U. S. Marshals, and 6000 U. S. troops from the 82nd Airborne who had flown into DC from Fort Bragg. Some of these soldiers had been deployed to Detroit in late July after President Johnson authorized their use to combat what was perceived and designated as an urban insurrection. Whatever its designation, those several days in July that engulfed the city led to scores of civilian deaths, thousands of arrests, and massive destruction.

Still wary of what would transpire at the March on the Pentagon, Frank could not imagine anywhere near the levels of violence that rocked Detroit this past summer. Although the government was preparing for and even predicting mindless chaos, he kept on assuring himself that the commitment to nonviolence enunciated by the March organizers and reflective of his own orientation would inform all the events of the day. Little did he suspect that he and so many other demonstrators would be overtaken by the spontaneous eruption of minor acts of aggression. By the end of Saturday night after hours of occupying the Pentagon Plaza, Frank would experience a sadistic whack from a white-helmeted red-faced Marshal as he tried to protect the young woman next to him from being yanked up by that same Marshal and treated even more viciously. His encounter with one of the soldiers late in the evening produced repeated boot kicks in his back while having water dumped on his head.

Although these minor injuries caused Frank momentary pain, they could not possibly rival the lethal pain and death the U. S. government was inflicting on the Vietnamese at the very same time he had received his blows. In Quang Tri province on the border between North and South Vietnam, B-52 bombers were pulverizing several villages. (By the end of the war with the total tonnage of bombs unleashed by the Pentagon on Vietnam exceeding three times the amount expended by the Americans in World War II, only 11 of the 3500 villages in Quang Tri were unscathed.) A number of innocent Vietnamese peasants were being arrested and tortured as part of the CIA-sponsored Operation Phoenix. Tons of Agent Orange were being dropped not only on jungle regions where Viet Cong fighters were buried in their caves, away from the defoliation, while GIs downwind were absorbing the toxins, but also on rice paddies withering under the chemical assault. And jets added to the chemical assault by strafing villages with napalm, resulting in women and children suffering severe burns that would either kill them or scar them for life.

Frank would carry his own scars, mostly from the photographic and television images that laid bare the lie that the war in Vietnam was being fought to win "the hearts and minds" of the Vietnamese people. It was the victimized Vietnamese who had won his heart and mind to such an extent that he was willing to risk arrest, imprisonment, and maybe even his life to stop the further victimization of the people of Southeast Asia by a government that claimed it was operating with his consent. Everywhere he could, starting with the draft, he would withdraw that putative consent. As far as Frank was concerned, any compliance with this illegitimate authority should be confronted with resistance.

It was these rebellious thoughts that flooded his consciousness as the bus carrying him and the other 50 prospective protestors from Minnesota pulled into a church parking lot in Southeast Washington, D.C. on the late Saturday morning of October 21, 1967. Weary from the lack of sleep but propelled forward by the adrenaline rush of anticipation, Frank trudged into the church's basement. There he found coffee, donuts, and fruit spread out on several tables. Pouring himself some watery black coffee, he was welcomed by one of the Black women dispensing a flyer that contained a small map of the area, directions to the Lincoln Memorial, and telephone numbers for legal and medical aid. She also pointed out a cloakroom where he could, if he wished, leave his backpack and any other belongings.

Unburdening himself of the backpack but not his discordant thoughts, Frank was impatient to get over to the

Reflecting Pool where other demonstrators had begun to congregate as they waited for the official rally to begin. He would have to wait for the other two buses from Minnesota to arrive and allow their passengers the opportunity to freshen up and partake of the offered repast. By the time all 150 were jammed into the church basement, noshing and jabbering away, the coordinator of the Minnesota contingent began barking out instructions about getting back on the buses for the short drive to an area around the Lincoln Memorial. Emphasizing, in particular, the need to be back on the buses no later than 7 P.M. for the trip back to the Twin Cities, he also recommended leaving belongings on the bus since they wouldn't be coming back to the church. Frank disregarded these instructions since he had planned to meet up with friends from Madison later Saturday evening and ride back with them to Wisconsin. From there he would take the bus or hitch to Minneapolis.

Of course, the best-laid plans often go awry. Given the swirl of events, minor mishaps, and compelling conflicts that emerged later in the day and into the evening, Frank would miss those connections and wind up hitching back from D.C. all the way to Minneapolis, managing in the process to get one long ride from Maryland to Mankato, Minnesota. That adventure, however, became a mere footnote to the main narrative of the day, one charged with highs and lows and splitting Frank into multiple personalities as he was carried along by the disparate and desperate actions of the March on the Pentagon.

Along with his fellow Minnesotans, Frank boarded the bus for its short trip to a locale in the vicinity of the Lincoln Memorial reserved for those large out-of-state vehicles. Up and down the crowded street, a variety of buses were disgorging their passengers, all of whom were streaming toward the Reflecting Pool. Some carried homemade signs on which could be seen brightly colored messages, reflective of the slogans for the day: "Confront the War-Makers! March on the Pentagon!" A few others, in the spirit of high-minded hippiedom, had fashioned pictographic representations of the Pentagon being levitated. Several placards, bearing the starkly simple, but glaringly red-lettered word in all caps, RESIST, bobbed above the heads of the mostly youthful demonstrators as they made their way to the assembled gathering.

As Frank approached the crowd, he could hardly make out the words being uttered by one of the speakers on the erected podium in front of the Lincoln Memorial. Moving forward by slicing through the throng, he reached a position on the left flank that allowed him to hear whatever harangues emanated from the stage. It also provided him a perch to look towards Virginia even though he was unable to see the objective of today's march. Although he could just make out the figure of the young Black man who now was addressing the restless assembly, he clearly heard the words being bellowed out by that speaker: "White people are just beginning to find out what it's like to have grievances and not be able to influence the government. We must resist. We must resist." And those who heard his shout, responded, "Resist, Resist!" To which the Black orator now added, "Hell, no, we won't go!" And, again, those within hearing distance took up the cry of "Hell, no, we won't go!"

Just at that moment, as if to punctuate that chant by an ironic action, the left flank detached itself from the assembled and started sprinting towards the Arlington Memorial Bridge.

Out in front of this detachment were the fluttering red, blue, and yellow flags of the NLF. Dashing across the bridge, the vanguard reached the temporary fencing constructed to keep out the very hordes that now descended on the fringes of the Pentagon. Making short shrift of the wire barrier, hundreds pushed their way onto the mall of the Pentagon. With Frank following their lead, the charged-up crowd now raced onto the Pentagon's plaza only to be met with hundreds of MPs and U.S. marshals. Instead of advancing any further, the marchers, elated by their penetration of the Pentagon defenses but wary of the forces arrayed now against them, sat down and began their nonviolent siege of this hated symbol of U.S. militarism and war-making.

Frank found himself wedged in between this contingent of like-minded and youthful seated protestors and the phalanx of young uniformed MPs standing upright on the steps of the Pentagon. Just behind the MPs were the white-helmeted older U. S. Marshals, glaring out at what they regarded as the worst examples of degenerate youth, bent on destruction of the American way of life. For these recently deputized Virginia rednecks that way of life was rooted in white supremacy and male chauvinism. That's probably why one of these Marshals, spying a white woman nuzzling next to her Black boyfriend at the edge of the steps, became agitated. Finding an opening between two burly MPs, the even heavier-set Marshal reached over and grabbed the woman. Close enough to where the Marshal had pulled her up, Frank instinctively arose and latched on to her arm. Releasing the distraught female, the Marshal thrust his baton into Frank's side, toppling him backward into the extended arms of a few of the seated demonstrators.

Alarmed that he might be injured, a few others stood to move Frank back, away from any more aggression from the arrayed authorities.

As he was ferried further away from the front and moving about on his feet, Frank experienced a strong urge to urinate. The only possible site for relieving himself was to scurry into the bushes along the side of the Pentagon. Although some of the more militant revelers among the marchers had joked about pissing on the Pentagon, as opposed to levitating it, Frank had never even entertained such a transgressive idea. However, now confronted with the reality of the situation, he unzipped and pissed on one of the bleached white walls, turning it temporarily yellow. If only this little stream could become a roaring torrent, a rushing yellow river that would submerge the Pentagon, Frank would then be truly relieved.

Wending his way out of the bushes and back onto the crowded plaza, Frank could hear someone nearby talking into a bullhorn. The sandy-haired speaker, wearing old army fatigues, addressed his words in particular to the soldiers who had taken up positions on the outer perimeter of the plaza. He described his participation in military operations in Vietnam and the growing disillusionment he and some of his comrades-in-arms experienced as a result of those operations. Interrupted initially by one of the commanding officers with a bullhorn of his own, barking out orders for holding the line and not allowing anyone to come or go, the persistent and calming voice of the Vietnam Vet vanquished the effort by this officer to distract the attention of his men. If none of those troops were moved by the confessional monologue of this earnest veteran, Frank certainly was.

When the Vietnam Vet relinquished the bullhorn, there was a momentary break before the invisible officer's orders were repeated – "Company B, Hold the Line. No One Comes. No One Goes." In response, a few among the seated protestors began singing "America, the Beautiful." With the lyrics invoking "purple mountain majesties" and more voices joining in the first and only verse sung, a number of young men stood up with draft cards in hand. Passing around a lighter, the draft cards were torched among a new brotherhood of resisters as dusk began to envelop all who enacted these remarkable moments on the Pentagon's plaza.

The singing and draft card burning for some of the demonstrators marked a bittersweet conclusion to the day's activities. For Frank, it was another episode in the longer drama of the Pentagon siege. Determined to stay through the night even in the face of dwindling numbers, his sit-in was now joined by an old friend from Pitt. Frank and his undergrad buddy kept up their spirits by reminiscing while encroaching soldiers were beginning to use their boots to break up the sit-down. After receiving some kicks to their spines and having water dumped on their heads, both he and his friend decided it was time to depart.

Walking together back over the Arlington Memorial Bridge, they exchanged what each regarded as the highlights of the march. Frank surprised himself with what could only be described as enacting multiple personalities throughout the day, from militant protestor to merry prankster to earnest nonviolent moral witnessing. Finding their way in the dark to where some of the buses were still parked, his friend was thankful that the Chicago bus had not yet departed. However, the Minnesota buses were long gone. Because Frank needed to return to the church to collect his belongings, he reluctantly said goodbye to his college buddy, expressing his regret to miss spending more time together and a ride to the Windy City.

Frank removed the paper he had been given earlier in the day from his back pocket. Slightly wet, he could still make out the directions to where the church was located. Although alone now and unsure of the neighborhoods he would be traversing, he managed to navigate the streets of Southeast D.C. with the occasional wave to the mostly Black residents enjoying their late Saturday evening. Consulting the map, he eventually arrived at the church, tired from the walk and the events of the day.

Fifteen

OCTOBER 22, 1967

Frank dragged his weary body across the Washington Avenue Bridge as students, now clad in lightweight jackets, passed him on either side, rushing to their mid-morning Monday classes. He had been in transit for over twenty-four hours. Luckily, his ride from Takoma Park, Maryland to Mankato, Minnesota with a newly appointed Assistant Professor in the Mankato State History Department also included crashing at the rented apartment this bearded fellow demonstrator inhabited. Sharing the driving over the long haul back to Minnesota, they also spent many hours recounting their experiences at the March on the Pentagon. They arrived at the Mankato apartment around 2 A.M. on Monday, exhausted from both the road trip and the reliving of certain terrifying moments from the demonstration. Not even bothering to remove his now battle-tested jeans, Frank flung himself on the sleek new Danish modern couch that his host wearily designated for sleeping. After a few short hours of relative restlessness, he quietly departed for the nearby Mankato bus station.

As he was walking in the early morning light towards the depot, Frank encountered a large granite monument. Carved on its face were the words: "Here Were Hanged 38 Sioux Indians: Dec. 26th, 1862." Although aware of the long and brutal history of what came to be known as "Indian Removal," also known as ethnic cleansing, also known as genocide, he was not at all cognizant of the specific incidents in the United States war against the Dakota Sioux that led to this hanging. Only later when he did some research did he discover that over 300 Dakota warriors were condemned to die after defending their land from the invasion of white settlers. In reducing that number to 38, President Lincoln signed off on the largest mass execution in U. S. history. Fifty years after the hanging, the prominent white citizens of Mankato erected the monument as their own contribution to the civic order of white supremacy. (After years of protest by Native American activists, the memorial to that awful event would finally be removed in 1972.)

During the three-hour bus ride from Mankato to Minneapolis, Frank alternated between a fitful sleep and an enraged arousal about the past political landscape of this state, this country, and its connection to the Vietnam War. Wasn't the mass murder of Native peoples on the North American continent a prelude to the imperial slaughter now unfolding in Southeast Asia? For the U. S. Generals who fought these wars weren't they, at some psychological level, about going into "Indian Territory" and wiping out the natives? All, of course, done in the heroic quest to advance civilization!

When he finally arrived at the Minneapolis bus station, he trudged the mile or so back to the West Bank house that he and Mary now occupied together. Although Mary had given him Betty's key, he had forgotten it in his rush to board the D.C. bound bus last Friday. Hoping that Mary was still at home, he knocked on the dilapidated, but still functioning, side door with its splotches of peeled paint. The poor excuse for an entry way swung open, revealing the pajama-clad fetching young woman with whom he now shared his lust, his love, and his life. They embraced as if he had been absent for years and held each other without a word spoken for several minutes.

"I was so worried. Why didn't you call me and let me know what had happened to you."

Embarrassed that he hadn't even taken the time to use a pay phone at one of the rest stops on the road trip back, he muttered, "Sorry."

"Are you hungry?"

"I'm starved, but I'd like to take a shower first before I have to get to American Studies Seminar."

"Why don't you just catch up on some sleep after the shower. I'll take notes for us both."

"Thanks. I'd probably be a zombie at the seminar."

Dropping his backpack on the tatty rust-colored lounger in their diminutive living room, Frank slumped onto the equally shabby small couch. Mary curled up next to him, reluctant to pepper him with the myriad questions she wanted to pose about the march and all that had transpired in the three days of his absence. Instead, she told him something that she immediately regretted when it escaped her mouth.

"A Dow recruiter is going to be on campus tomorrow for two days."

"What? Jesus Christ! Is anyone organizing a protest?"

"Well, I think Bob Sagan from SDS posted a leaflet around campus calling for a demonstration for Tuesday morning when this recruiter shows up at the Placement Office."

"As soon as I shower and eat something, I'll run over to the TCDAC office and write up a flyer that we can hand out when we block the entrance to the Placement Office tomorrow."

"For God's sake, Frank," Mary sputtered, "Can't you take a break? You just spent the last week in non-stop anti-draft and antiwar demonstrations. Shouldn't you recuperate a little before leaping into your next action?"

He sighed, knowing that she had presented a compelling case for him to let others engage in this fight. Yet, he couldn't shake the strong sense that he had a responsibility to show up, especially against the evil corporate manufacturer of napalm.

Almost pleading with her, Frank, channeling Gary Cooper's role as Sheriff Will Kane in *High Noon*, replied, "I've got to go, Mary."

Rising angrily from the couch, Mary didn't bother facing him as she spat out, "I really don't want to live with someone who has a martyr complex!'

Before he could reply, she strode into the bedroom and slammed the door behind her.

Too tired to continue arguing and too unsure of the complicated reasons for rushing into another demonstration, Frank leaned back on the sofa and closed his eyes.

Instead of the dark emptiness of sleep lulling him into unconsciousness, the starkly graphic images of napalmed

Vietnamese doused his now inflamed consciousness and conscience.

Shedding his wrinkled smelly clothes, he snatched a towel from the bathroom and walked around to the adjacent brick shower stall. Built as an add-on without any heating source, taking a shower during any months other than those of the steamy summer ones was hardly a leisurely, or even comfortable, endeavor. Nonetheless, Frank let the warm water wash over him, holding back the tears that were welling up in his eyes. He turned off the water and the tears with renewed resolve.

Drying off and then wrapping the towel around his waist, he tiptoed over to the bedroom door and gently knocked a few times.

"Mary, please let me in. I need to get dressed and get going."

She opened the door, but said nothing. Glaring at him as he dressed, her anger, however, soon melted away. "Perhaps, I'll join you sometime tomorrow for part of the demonstration."

"That would be great. Would you mind bringing some food with you? I'm not sure how long we'll be there."

She nodded her assent and walked over to where the now fully dressed Frank stood. Whatever tensions had emerged earlier had now dissipated and their libidinal desires overwhelmed the previous chilly separation. Mary took the lead in undressing him as Frank pulled off her pajamas. Naked, the pair tumbled into bed and plunged into the waves of passion that now swallowed them up.

Sixteen

Frank awoke first. Breathing lightly next to him, Mary seemed sound asleep. He tried not to disturb her as he rose from the bed. Having spent most of the afternoon and evening yesterday at the TCDAC office writing out and mimeographing a flyer for today's protest against the presence of a Dow Chemical recruiter on the University of Minnesota campus, he wanted to distribute the copies as soon as the Placement Office opened. Dressing quickly, he made sure to wear his one sport coat in order to convey the image of a respectable and responsible grad student.

While he was rummaging about in the combined kitchen and dining room looking for a bowl and the cereal to pour into it, Mary groggily called out to him, "The cereal is in the pantry." The little hole-in-the-wall that comprised the pantry was barely large enough to fit the five-shelf wire rack into which had been placed a wide variety of canned and package goods.

"Found it," Frank yelled back to Mary as he took a large box of *Wheaties* off the top shelf. Ah, the "Breakfast of Champions." He had been a middling long-distance runner in high school and college, but hardly in the pantheon of great athletes who graced the box covers of the cereal he held in his hand. What about a "Breakfast of Chumpions," for those of us who continued to buy this overpriced product because it gave us a temporary boost of energy and ego? While Frank derisively dismissed the fantasies embedded in the advertising gimmick for *Wheaties*, he did enjoy a morning bowl of whole-wheat flakes even though it was packaged for celebrity-starved consumers.

After finishing the cereal and placing the now empty bowl in the sink, he went over to the bathroom to brush his teeth. He didn't want to have any residue of the morning breakfast drawing attention away from the righteous rants that he intended to discharge in the direction of any and all students who either attempted to enter the Placement Office or were merely passing by. Frank also counted on his fellow protestors to distribute the flyers that he was bringing with him in his backpack.

He returned to the bedroom to retrieve the house key that he had left on the dresser and to say goodbye to Mary, especially now that she was in the process of awakening.

"Just thought I'd give you a quick kiss before I leave."

"That would be appreciated. Hope to see you later after my "Nineteenth Century American Fiction" class."

"Well, you can call me Ishmael when you see me again."

"Just don't get caught up in trying to harpoon any whales, no matter what their color."

Frank chuckled at their lame repartee. Planting a kiss on Mary's luscious lips, he exited the bedroom, snatched his backpack from the chair, and pushed open the door to the brisk outside air.

Striding quickly, his walk across the Washington Avenue Bridge was unimpeded at this early hour by the streams of students who later would jam the pathway in their rush to get to class. Under the bridge the waters of the Mississippi River calmly flowed, oblivious to the adrenaline-induced turmoil that coursed through Frank's wiry body. He anticipated a day of confrontation. However, he was unsure of who would be prevented from entering the Placement Office or how long the disruption would continue without intervention by university authorities or police.

When Frank entered the Liberal Arts Building where the intended protest was to take place, he saw ahead a dozen or so students already milling about in front of the Placement Office. He knew several of the demonstrators, including Bob Sagan who had strategically situated himself in front of the door.

"Hey, Bob, has the Dow recruiter shown up yet?"

"Unfortunately, he must have arrived super early and is now somewhere inside. No students have attempted to go in to interview as far as we know."

"If you want to keep standing, I'll sit down and stretch my legs across the doorway as a bodily blockade. I just don't want to get into any physical altercation with students in particular. I do, however, want to make them stop and think about what Dow does and what the war is all about."

Bob nodded and began to sing the chorus from Buffalo Springfield's song, "For What It's Worth" – "We better stop, hey, what's that sound/Everybody look what's going down." The other demonstrators joined in and soon there was a loud sing-a-long echoing around the halls. Additional students, attracted by the noise, did stop to see what was going down. This allowed Frank the opportunity to hand out the leaflet which explained the reason for the demonstration against the Dow recruiter, what napalm was and how it was used in the war in Southeast Asia, and why students should condemn the university for its complicity in providing Dow with access to potential employees.

It wasn't too long before the first of those potential employees showed up at the Placement Office door. Glowering at Frank, whose legs were splayed out to approximate a sawhorse wooden barrier, this crew-cut athletic-looking student seemed on the verge of plowing through what he regarded as a pathetic nuisance. Before he made his move, Bob grabbed the unsuspecting guy by the waist and a brief tussle ensued. Frank jumped to his feet and tried to separate the two antagonists by attempting to insert himself in between the two bodies. With all three stepping back from further physical conflict, there was a pause that Frank used to launch his diatribe against Dow.

Before he could make his moral appeal, the now slightly frazzled student yelled out angrily: "You assholes are denying me my freedom of choice. I have a right to go into this office and you have no right to deny me entry."

"Look," Frank coolly responded. "if you want to go in and offer yourself to Dow Chemical, knowing what napalm does, how it's been used, and why Dow and this war are so immoral, go ahead."

Swatting aside these points as if they were irritating and ultimately impotent insects, the guy pushed aside Frank and Bob and entered the Placement Office. Frank resisted the temptation to call out after him that in meeting with Dow this student had become complicit in corporate malevolence. And if this eager recruit went on to work for Dow, he would become, as Marcuse wrote in *One Dimensional Man*, one of the "slaves of industrial civilization," reduced to "an instrument" of the policy and practice of war-making production.

As Frank sat back down in the doorway, he noticed that the number of his fellow protestors had grown. There were now about two dozen students lining the hallway. Reaching into his backpack, he pulled out the leaflets and urged those nearby to pass them around. One young female student, seated among those demonstrating against Dow, began to improvise on the lyrics for "We Shall Overcome." With intensity and clarity, she sang "No More Children Burned." The others soon repeated the new wording. After exhausting that song, another civil rights anthem, "We Shall Not Be Moved," was taken up by the animated and expanding group. Within the next hour, the size of the protest, consisting of almost fifty students, constituted a formidable blockade to either entrance to or egress from the Placement Office.

Appearing at the doorway to that office was one of the university counselors, looking rather forlorn in his rumpled suit. With a scrunched up face, he turned to the still standing Bob and pleaded to be allowed out in order to go to the bathroom.

Both Bob and Frank took pity on the fellow and moved aside. As he wedged past them, he asked whether he would be allowed to return.

"Guess what," Bob said with a jolly face and sly smile, "you've got the rest of the day off."

"Now wait a second here, young man," the university employee remonstrated, "you've got to let me back in."

"Take it up with your Dean or the President. They should have never given Dow Chemical permission to come onto campus. They are the ones responsible for the disruption in your daily routine. Alternatively, you could either join us or offer to escort the Dow recruiter out of the office. For that, we would gladly let you back in."

The counselor just shook his head and hurried off to the bathroom.

Seeing a breech in the barrier, another student snuck by Bob and Frank. Looking somewhat disconsolate about letting their guard down, they decided on a new sentinel tactic. They wouldn't try to prevent anyone entering or exiting the Placement Office. They would, however, ask each person whether they had a "permission slip" from Malcolm Moos, the President of the University, to attend a recruiting session with the Dow representative. If not, they would direct them to the President's office in Morrill Hall. A few students trying to enter to interview with the Dow recruiter did get thoroughly confused by this tactic and left without entering.

The morale of the protesting group remained high even after hours of hanging around the Placement Office. Later in the afternoon, Mary showed up with several others, carrying bags of bagels and apples that she and her compatriots handed out to the seated demonstrators. When it was announced that the recruiting session was over and the door would be shut, there was a heated discussion about how to proceed. It was Frank who suggested they march over to Morrill Hall where the administration offices were and attempt to occupy the President's Office. Enthusiastically endorsed by nearly everyone, they rose as a collective body and began the short procession to the Administration Building.

Although some of the protestors decided to drop out of the next confrontational move, several score continued, including Frank, Mary, and Bob in the lead. Marching up the steps to Morrill Hall, they reached the President's Office. Finding that closed and the Regents Conference room next door unlocked, they swarmed into the administrative headquarters and sat down. To Mary's surprise, Frank announced to the group that he would begin a fast as a way to express compassion for the innocent victims of the napalm produced by Dow Chemical and condemnation of the university's complicity in this war crime. (A reporter who had been trailing along with the demonstrators would include this announcement when he filed his story with the *Minneapolis Star*.)

Mary pulled Frank aside and with a frazzled worried look on her face expressed her displeasure that he had unilaterally made the decision to go on a hunger strike. Trying to calm her concern, he assured her that it would be limited to twenty-four hours. In fact, Frank wound up engaging in this tactic for forty-eight hours and experiencing during the last twelve a range of bizarre hallucinations, including one where he had turned into an insect that was then doused with the Dow pesticide, chlorpyrifos. In the final hours of the hunger strike, with the *Doors* song, "People Are Strange" ricocheting around his head, Frank wondered how Gandhi had managed to carry out so many of his much longer fasts without going a little crazy.

As Frank, Mary, and a dozen or so others settled in for an extended occupation of the Regents Office, the door from the President's Office suddenly opened. There stood Malcolm Moos, the President of the University of Minnesota and a former speechwriter for President Eisenhower, flanked by some Deans and two campus cops. Moos was reputed to have been the author of Eisenhower's famous "Farewell Address" where he warned about the "unwarranted influence of the military-industrial complex." Frank made sure to have a reference to that part of Eisenhower's speech in the Dow leaflet as a rebuke to Moos and what amounted to the expansion of that complex to a military-industrial-academic one. Surveying the room and the remaining student protestors, Moos offered to meet with "the leader."

Springing to his feet, animated by an anarchist spirit, Frank asserted: "We have no leader! We are all leaders!"

At that point, Moos turned on his heel and re-entered his presidential sanctum. The two cops, looking like a more somber version of Laurel and Hardy, remained behind. Apparently, they were to keep watch on the ragtag group in case there was a sudden urge to vandalize the room. Not only were the students averse to any destructive behavior, but they were also already pairing up to simulate an impulse to "make love, not war." For Mary and Frank this meant crawling under the large conference room table and making out. One could almost hear the Hardy cop muttering under his breath, "This is another fine mess you've gotten me into."

After a restless night of intermittent heavy petting and nodding off, Frank and Mary rolled out from their temporary "love nest." With loud yawns, they and the other students tried to shake off their drowsiness and address the next phase of the Dow protest. Since they knew that the Dow recruiter was scheduled to conduct interviews in the Business Administration Building on the West Bank of the campus, they readied themselves for the march across the bridge. Mary let Frank know that she would continue walking back to their place, rest for a little, and then go to her afternoon class. She hoped to see Frank later that evening. He mumbled something about another possible sit-in/sleep-in to which Mary responded with a vexed sigh.

"You promised you would only do a twenty-four hour hunger strike. I assumed that meant you would be home later tonight. Are you going to break your promise to me?"

Glancing furtively at Mary, Frank hemmed-and-hawed. Before he could use the obvious excuse of the war necessitating extraordinary behavior on his part, Mary lodged her just complaint, "The war shouldn't provide a pretext for negating the pledge you made to me."

"I don't believe I told you I wouldn't continue with the demonstration."

"Fine," she angrily replied. "Go on with your martyrdom. Just don't always expect me to be a willing enabler."

Frank sheepishly regarded her pursed lips. She stared back at him, daring him to say something that she could pounce on. He chose not to open his mouth. Gathering his backpack, he waved at the other students to follow him out the door. Mary waited for them to exit and then, with ample space between her and the group, she ambled down the steps of Morrill Hall, out onto the Quad, and in the direction of the bridge and her West Bank domicile where another round of domestic and political dispute roiled their household.

Seventeen

LATE OCTOBER 1967

Frank didn't return home that evening. It wasn't until the following morning that he staggered through the door to their West Bank residence. Startled, Mary spun around from the stove where she had been cooking some oatmeal. Neither moved until Frank offered his apology.

"I should have listened to you, Mary, especially about limiting the hunger strike to twenty-four hours. I've been hallucinating all through the night and missing you at the same time."

"I guess it might not mean anything to say that I was worried."

"Of course, it means everything to me."

"Are you ready to slow down, take a breather, and maybe pay more attention to your courses, and an actual social life?"

After the last very intense ten days of almost non-stop demonstrations, Frank regarded Mary's question and advice as perfectly reasonable. Still, he couldn't suppress the feeling that he wasn't entitled to withdraw from the political engagements that his conscience compelled him to undertake. So, he hedged his assent to Mary's request.

"Okay. But I can't really absent myself from work at the TCDAC, especially as a consequence of our anti-draft activities and planning for more in the future."

Mary pondered how to respond. She didn't want to deny Frank working with his fellow draft resisters. On the other hand, she was fearful that it would consume so much of his time, becoming, in the process, an obsessive quest.

"Can you try to restrict the amount of hours that you spend over there in the office and on related matters?"

"Yeh. I'll work out a schedule with the guys and check with you about any road trips."

"Thanks. Now, do you want some of this hot oatmeal?"

Snatching a bowl from the cupboard, Frank approached Mary like a begging supplicant. She smiled beatifically and ladled the oatmeal into the receptacle he held in his quivering hands. Her grace shone upon him even as he wolfed down the contents of the bowl and slurped up every last morsel of the oatmeal.

"More, please?" sounding a little like a grown-up Oliver Twist. Fortunately, for Frank, Mary did not wield her ladle like an instrument of punishment, but rather as an implement of mercy. After he finished inhaling the second helping, he slumped in the chair, gazed at Mary, and thanked his lucky stars for this compassionate companion.

"I have to get going to class," Mary said.

"I'm going to rest and then catch up on reading for my American Intellectual History seminar tonight. Maybe we can have an early dinner before I have to drive over to St. Paul to Professor Wellborn's house for the evening class?"

"Sounds good to me."

As Mary was gathering her own books for her late morning literature course, Frank watched in silence. He rose and then advanced to where she was busying herself with preparations for leaving. He reached out and encircled her with his arms, nuzzling his lips into her hair.

"Don't have time for this now, Mister. But maybe when I return, we can tickle each other's fancy."

"I look forward to that," he gleefully exclaimed even as he admitted to himself that he was not quite sure where Mary's fancy was physically located. However, he looked forward to the exploration of her body to find it.

His own body, replenished with a modest intake of food, cried out for decent rest. More pressing, after getting a whiff of his malodorous scent, would be a refreshing and cleansing shower. Quickly shedding his unkempt clothes, he entered the confined space where the watery spray helped him both decontaminate and decompress. After toweling off, he didn't feel like dressing again. So, he put on Mary's tight-fitting orange terrycloth bathrobe, lay down on the bed, and picked up *From Caligari to Hitler* by Siegfried Kracauer, the assigned book for tonight's class.

Like much of Professor Wellborn's seminar, the Kracauer text seemed so contrary to what Frank imagined for this advanced course in American Intellectual History. It wasn't only the readings that were somewhat idiosyncratic. The seminar itself, consisting of about a dozen grad students, took place at Professor Wellborn's home where he conducted the class lying on his back on the floor in the middle of his living room. Although he claimed this was because of an injury to his spine, his supine position, ironically, enabled an elevated tone to the whole evening discussion.

As he read Kracauer's interpretation of how certain cinematic characters prefigured the rise of Hitler, he fixated on the description of how Caligari stood for "unlimited authority that idolizes power as such, and, to satisfy the lust for domination ruthlessly violates all human rights and values." Eventually, he drifted off to a troubled sleep, riddled with the resonant images from Kracauer's book. Instead of the backdrop of Weimar Germany, Frank pictured a future nightmarish American environment where a frightening political tyrant, not unlike Caligari, sought to dominate and wreak havoc on the country. Although buffoonish, this fat Orange Menace threatened all who refused to bow down before him. Dragged in front of this evil demon, Frank felt a dread unlike any he had ever experienced and raised his voice in a howl for help.

Hearing the shriek, Mary entered the bedroom and shook Frank awake. When he opened his eyes and caught site of her angelic face, he knew he was saved if only from this horrific dream.

"You must have had a nightmare."

"Definitely. Just a bad dream."

"Well, you slept a long time. I came home and saw how you had curled up in the bed with my bathrobe and that book and decided not to disturb you."

"You mean there's no time to tickle each other's fancy?"

"That will have to wait until after you get back from class for which, by the way, you're going to be late unless you hurry to get there. I made a sandwich you can take with you so you can eat on the way over to St. Paul."

Dressing now in his own better fitting clothes, Frank took the proffered food, stuffed the Kracauer book in the backpack, gave Mary a smack on her lips and exited the house. Jumping into the driver's seat in the Corvair, he maneuvered the car to the cross-town highway towards St. Paul.

Eighteen

LATE OCTOBER 1967

Having recovered his academic groove and promising Mary to catch up on all the course assignments, Frank headed off to the TCDAC office. He intended to volunteer for whatever tasks were paramount and where his limited talents could be put to good use. With Halloween around the corner, he started fantasizing about ways to spook the overwhelmingly white, middle class, and elderly members of the various local draft boards or using a giant Jack-O-Lantern as the repository for another draft card turn-in or burning. While the week of October 16-20 witnessed a total of nearly 3000 draft cards being returned or burned, that amount was only one percent of the projected total inductees for 1967. There was already planning for an April anti-draft action. Nonetheless, the TCDAC would have to expand its efforts to build for even larger draft resistance events for all of 1968 and beyond.

As Frank climbed the stairs to the TCDAC, he could hear loud voices emanating from the office. From outside the room, it sounded like a spirited discussion about strategy and tactics.

When he entered, the arguments abated and all warmly welcomed him into their fellowship circle. The stalwarts were gathered round with Dan Whitman acting as an informal mediator. Jim Penny scowled at John Rider who kept on shaking his head, seemingly at odds with the gruff demeanor of Penny. Hanging back was Fred Adamson, a little bowled over by the intensity of the debate that preceded Frank's arrival.

Embarrassed that he may have interceded at an extremely delicate moment, the bewildered grad student hesitatingly apologized for the interruption.

"No need to act contrite," Jim hammered at him. "We were just having a disagreement about who should go on the journey north for speaking engagements at a church in St. Cloud and at St. John's University."

John barged right in with his own explanation of the dispute. "Look, it's not any church in St. Cloud. It's the massive Rivendale Methodist Church and I think Fred brings the right credentials to accompany Dan as our representatives. No disrespect to you, Jim, but they probably provide the best balance for our presentation."

Jim harrumphed in response while Fred blushed.

John continued to make his case about the composition of the trio for the journey. "And St. John's asked me specifically because of family up there and the Catholic connection."

Although late to all the fine points in the debates, Frank had to admit that John had logic on his side. Then, again, the only argument he heard from Jim was a guttural sound.

"Any chance, Frank, you can come in over the weekend to help Jim and his sister Eileen with mailings, calls, and any visits?"

"Sure, no problem." As soon as he answered, he realized he would have to talk to Mary about all the plans for the weekend. He knew they were going to a party at some friends of hers on Saturday night. Still, that would leave time during the day unless there was something else that she had in mind. He certainly did not want to create any more friction with Mary unless, of course, it was of a certain bodily kind.

With a rough consensus achieved, the trio undertook a series of preparations for their passage up north. Meanwhile, Frank joined Jim at the mimeograph machine for printing off letters they would start mailing on the weekend to the public lists of potential draftees. Jim remained somewhat disconsolate. Grumbling to himself and muttering a list of names, the squat fellow draft resister finally bellowed a discernable name.

"Balin."

"What, who is Balin?" Frank inquired.

"My great uncle Martin Balin. He was always just called by his last name from the time he worked underground in the mines in the Iron Range. He retired and moved to St. Cloud where he had some friends who have mostly passed away. Now, he's just an irascible old man with a long white beard. But that's who I wanted to visit on the journey up north."

"Wait, he's got the same name as one of the singers for the band, Jefferson Airplane. I have their album, *Surrealistic Pillow*. Have you heard of the band and the album?"

"I don't have time or tolerance for pop music. Maybe it's just my heritage from a long line of underground men who take no delight in trivial folderol."

"You might appreciate the song, 'Somebody to Love,' especially the opening lines, 'When the truth is found/To be Lies.'"

"Well, it's for sure that Sauron's truths are nothing but lies."

"What, who's Sauron?"

"Never mind. Just my way of talking about the Selective Service System. Speaking of the SSS, couldn't you ask some of those students in SASS to help out this weekend?"

"I'll have to wait until I'm back on campus next week. There might be one or two who could come over to the office on an irregular basis."

"Yeh, apparently regularity or responsibility isn't one of the trademarks of you students."

"Whoa, why the diatribe against students? Weren't you a student before you dropped out?

"One of the reasons I dropped out was because I couldn't stand the phoniness of student life."

Now Jim was sounding like an older Holden Caulfield. Frank had no interest in getting into an argument with him on this or, for that matter, any other issue. Maybe on another occasion when Penny wasn't so obviously pissed off. Turning back to their more immediate task of running off anti-draft materials, the two found a comradely rhythm in conjunction with the operation of the mimeograph machine.

Nineteen

NOVEMBER 4, 1967

This was going to be a real change of pace, thought Frank. A Saturday night party with friends of Mary whom he hadn't yet met. From what she told him about the couple living at the end of the block in the new apartment complex, there probably would be much they shared in common. Mary's close friend, Bonnie Baker, now completing her master's degree in Social Work at the 'U,' was a veteran civil rights activist, having worked with C.O.R.E. (Congress of Racial Equality) in Mississippi in the tumultuous and scary summer of 1964. She had briefly met Mickey Schwerner and James Chaney in Jackson the month before the KKK murdered them, along with Andrew Goodman (no relation). Bonnie's husband, Vince Bourgeois, was in the last year of Law School at the 'U.' He was from a prominent French-Canadian family that had settled in Minneapolis generations ago. His father was a lawyer in a well-known liberal law firm with close connections to the DFL. (The Democratic Farmer Labor party was formed in 1944 when the Democratic party merged with the more radical Farmer Labor party. During the post-war period of anti-communist hysteria, many of the left elements from the Farmer Labor party were purged.)

"Did you remember to buy a bottle of wine for the party," Mary called out from the bedroom.

"Geez, I forgot. Can't we just bring some beer?"

"No," she emphatically exclaimed. "You don't bring beer as a 'house-warming' gift. Besides Bonnie doesn't drink beer. She prefers a good bottle of red wine, like a Zinfandel. Can you run over to the liquor store and get one?"

Frank had never heard of Zinfandel. In fact, if he imbibed a glass of wine at the party tonight, it would be his first drink ever of that kind of fancy alcoholic beverage. The only wine his family ever consumed was the sickly sweet Manischewitz that was served during Passover. As far as he was concerned, every drop of that terrible tasting medicinal wine felt like an additional plague that had to be re-enacted during the Pesach ceremony as a punishment for being a diasporic Jew. He may have also absorbed by ideational osmosis his father's bias against any wine that had a swanky name and label with a price that was twice as much as Manischewitz. In any case, he intended to stick with beer at the party.

Depositing his wallet in the pocket of the University of Pittsburgh letter jacket, Frank donned the outer garment and made a dash to the liquor store where he previously received the gifted six-pack. He certainly didn't expect another gesture of largesse, especially since the person behind the counter was not the same one who waited on him the only other time he shopped there. Frank tentatively approached the much younger and thinner clerk to inquire about Zinfandel wine.

"Do you want a California or French Zinfandel?"

Flummoxed by a choice he was unprepared to make, he responded, "How about giving me what you think is the better one?"

"OK. I'll grab the California Zin for ya."

Paying what seemed like an exorbitant price, he was, nonetheless, hoping that the purchase might impress his hosts for tonight's party. Mary was already waiting outside their house, aglow with bright red lipstick that matched the color of the corner stop sign.

He held up the bottle of wine with one hand and slipped his other hand into hers. She led the way to the nearby building where Vince and Bonnie resided. The door of their second floor apartment was decorated with a number of stickers that clearly indicated the political proclivities of the inhabitants inside. One of those decals contained the familiar slogan: "END THE WAR, NOW!" Another sticker lacked any words, but conveyed its meaning by the clasping of black and white hands.

Mary knocked on one of the spaces without any stickers. When the door opened, a very skinny dark-complexioned woman peeked around the corner and then pulled Mary into the entry. They embraced with obvious delight until Bonnie released the hug.

"So, you must be Frank. Mary's told me a lot about you already, but I want to know more. C'mon in."

Feeling incredibly welcomed, he handed over to Bonnie the bottle of wine.

"Thanks. I love a good Zin. I'll open it in your honor and give you a glass."

Not wanting to reject her hospitality, he followed her into the kitchen as Mary went into the crowded living room. She greeted many of those present, all of whom were unknown to Frank although Mary would make sure that by the end of the evening she had introduced him to everyone, including the tabby cat. The feline had made a beeline to him upon entering the kitchen, sniffing around his trousers as if he carried a secret stash of catnip.

"Oh, don't mind Fidel. He has to check out everyone who comes into our apartment. He'll move along shortly. In the meantime, here's your glass of wine."

Frank took the goblet with its dark red contents and waited for Bonnie to pour herself a drink of the Zinfandel. With a swift motion, she filled a small tumbler almost to the brim. Beckoning him to raise his glass, she offered a toast, followed by a loud "L'Chayim."

"So, Mary tells me you were in Friends of SNCC at the University of Pittsburgh. What did your chapter do?"

"A little of everything from a Freedom School to raising funds for the struggle in the South. Not anywhere near as exciting or as dangerous as your experience with C.O.R.E."

Bonnie took a gulp of her wine and an even longer gulp of air. It seemed to Frank that she was still deeply affected by that time in the South. However, before she had the opportunity to speak, another person came barreling into the kitchen. Heading straight to the refrigerator without even acknowledging Frank, the chiseled-faced intruder was obviously someone familiar enough with the setup that he knew where to find the special imported German beer he now held in his hand.

"Vince, you could at least have the common courtesy to say hello to our guest, Mary's new beau, Frank."

With a look that combined equal parts curiosity and contempt, Vince proceeded to denounce draft resistance as little more than moral witnessing. Unwilling to hear Frank's defense, the about-to-be-attorney with aquiline facial features started spouting his own analysis of the failures of the anti-draft and antiwar movements.

"Look, you guys think that you're going to move your average Joe to get behind these flamboyant actions like marching under NLF flags and blocking induction centers? If you are really interested in changing things, you've got to get into the unions. You've got to take over the DFL leadership and exercise real political power. Not these symbolic adventurist escapades."

Taken aback by this unremitting verbal onslaught, Frank had to pause before defending himself and his fellow draft resisters and antiwar activists.

"I suppose the fact that we are trying to organize students to stop their own complicity with the war machine and fight all the remnants of the military-industrial complex on campus may seem irrelevant to you but it certainly has disrupted the university and built an expanding base of youthful opponents of the war."

Ready with his next dismissal of Frank's argument, Vince waved his arms and shouted, "You guys are just playing in a sandbox. You'll never change the system with your infantile tactics."

"So you would have us drop out, become construction workers, and make our antiwar pleas to George Meany?"

"Yeh, you might actually learn a skill and get these guys on your side before they decide to beat your head in with a heavy wrench."

He felt like Vince was already bludgeoning him with argumentative assaults, reflective of a certain aloofness and law school sophistry. Although some of what Vince said would later be recognized as having the ring of truth, Frank was in no mood to continue the fruitless debate the lawyer-in-training was foisting on him. He also learned after the party when he told Mary about this intemperate encounter with Vince that she had been involved with him when they were both undergrads at the 'U.' He was relieved and somewhat vindicated when she told him she broke up with him because of his boorish arrogance.

Twenty

EARLY NOVEMBER TO EARLY
DECEMBER 1967

Although Vince's rapid-fire criticisms marred the Saturday night respite Frank sought, he found solace in Mary's intimate embraces later that evening and in the following weeks. Their relationship grew closer as they settled into a routine of studying and making love. She was much more conscientious about her course work. He, on the other hand, would skip classes or do only the minimum amount of work, making excuses in order to spend time at the TCDAC office and participate in antiwar activities.

Throughout November 1967 the war escalated. Wherever and whenever members of President Johnson's administration spoke in public, antiwar protestors harassed them. Over ten thousand demonstrators greeted Secretary of State Dean Rusk in New York City. Massed against them were one thousand police who used their clubs to prevent any intrusion into the Hilton Hotel where Rusk was speaking. In

St. Paul, Frank joined with hundreds who surrounded the hotel where Vice President Hubert Humphrey defended the murderous onslaught on Vietnam with the insipid and idiotic ideological argument that if the Commies weren't stopped in Southeast Asia, they would be on the West Coast. Lacking an air force and a large navy, it was hard to imagine how the North Vietnamese would mount such an attack on continental U.S. Then, again, it was the monolithic bogeyman that Humphrey and the supporters of the war deployed in order to frighten citizens into defending an indefensible policy.

At the St. Paul demonstration, Frank and one of his antiwar buddies managed to slip into the hotel and enter the ballroom where Humphrey was addressing the friendly audience. Standing in the back close to the exit doors, Frank and his partner yelled out as loudly as possible: "Humphrey, you are a war criminal!" Both Secret Service and St. Paul Police pounced on his friend while Frank escaped down the escalator and out one of the side doors of the hotel. His buddy later would be bailed out, charged only with disturbing the peace.

When Frank returned to the street outside, chaos reigned in front of the hotel. Someone among the protestors had pulled a fire alarm, resulting in several fire trucks wading into the unruly demonstrators. At this point, he and a few others retreated to where he had parked the Corvair. They piled into the car, expecting to make a quick getaway. The temperamental automobile was not compliant, refusing to budge until Frank muttered under his breath the magical incantation. The Corvair responded and the relieved driver and passengers headed back to Minneapolis.

The University of Minnesota campus continued to be roiled by protests in November. Two separate campaigns that month aimed to shatter any complacency about the daily war crimes being committed in Vietnam. One of those actions was a deliberately provocative promotion by Rudy Schreier of SASS and Bob Sagan of SDS to demonstrate the horrors of napalm by dousing a dog with a homemade version of the heinous weapon. Never intending to do such a horrific act, Schreier and Sagan contacted the media about the specific time and location of the action. When reporters and some outraged citizens showed up, the pair handed out actual photographs of napalmed Vietnamese children, noting that the outrage needed to be directed at those who prosecuted a war against innocent civilians.

Less provocative, but still media-focused, was Al Himmelfarb's operation to disseminate flyers around campus with just the date of "November 17." His idea, prefiguring the Yippie actions of Jerry Rubin and Abbie Hoffman, was to whip up the alarm of the university authorities that some dramatic and maybe even violent event would occur on that date. Instead, his coterie of comrades showed up with a tank of helium and a large number of balloons with the label "Stop the War!" Alternatively, using the helium to blow up the balloons and transform their voices into that of angry munchkins, the "November 17" escapade drifted, like the balloons, into the uncaring chilly air surrounding the campus.

The draft resister crew at the TCDAC, including Frank, was gearing up for another national day of draft card turn-ins on December 4[th.] Both Dan and Fred were working full-time in the office, producing a variety of materials that Frank and the others distributed throughout the Twin Cities. The ringing of the telephone was constant as nervous young men called for advice and, in some cases, for specific information about what were the best routes to Canada and what would happen to them if they left the country. Once Frank got such a request from an unidentified caller who sounded suspiciously older than the average TCDAC inquirer. Reluctant to give any advice that could open the Center to legal incrimination, he feigned ignorance and gave out the number to the Canadian Consul in St. Paul.

All the TCDAC efforts to create some momentum for a significant draft card turn-in on December 4 did have positive results. A march from the campus to the Old Federal Building in downtown Minneapolis was a spirited affair, culminating in several draft cards being burned. More importantly, a few of the new draft resisters became committed members of the TCDAC, enlarging, in the process, the fellowship. In particular, Fred Adamson gained a new roommate and helper by the name of Stan Gamson who followed Fred everywhere he went. In fact, in the aftermath of the December 4th action, Fred and Stan made plans to go to Moorhead, Minnesota and on to Fargo, North Dakota to deliver packages of anti-draft literature. Given the early snowfall, the perilous journey to Moorhead would be a real test of their endurance and ultimate quest.

Twenty-One

AUGUST 25, 1970

Both the driver and the passenger were tense as they approached their destination. Although Frank and the mysterious stranger had rehearsed their story ad nauseum, they were nervous as the Corvair slowly entered International Falls, Minnesota. They could see the Rainey River in the distance and the bridge that crossed from the U. S. side to Fort Frances, the small Canadian town that was their escape gateway. Even though it was a weekday, the hot August weather guaranteed that vacationers would be heading to the wilds of Ontario. They, of course, had a different route in mind.

The single lane that formed for the crossing moved slowly, exacerbating their apprehension.

"Get out your driver's license," said Frank as he pulled his own from the wallet he had placed in between his legs. "The customs agent will want to know our citizenship and then where we are going. Hopefully, that's all that we'll need to say." He shuddered to think about any other verbal exchange that could either poke holes in the fishing story or probe ever more deeply into what their background was.

Soon, the dusty beat-up Corvair was next in line. He could see the uniformed customs agent in a formal dark blue outfit with shiny brass buttons that reminded him of U. S. naval officers. If only this Canadian official acted less like someone in authority and more like a welcoming tourist guide, he would be able to relax.

Face to face with the youngish looking customs agent, Frank was relieved, believing that the youthfulness would indicate a more liberal attitude. However, the stern looking visage of this Canadian officer seemed to belie his age.

With an officious voice, the customs agent asked to see the licenses of both. Scrutinizing first Frank's face and then his driver's license, there was a brief pause and then the inquiry: "Okay, Franklin Roosevelt Goodman, if that's your real name, where are you going in Canada and how long will you be there?"

He was starting to sweat even more than what the hot weather induced.

Answering in a deliberate voice, Frank said, "We're going to meet some Canadian friends for a fishing trip on Rainey Lake. We'll just be there for two days."

"You want to show me your fishing gear," asked the dutifully inquisitive agent.

"We're going to use all the gear they have. So, we didn't have to bring any."

Turning now to the mysterious stranger, the Canadian official looked over to the passenger side and back to the license he held in his hand.

"Hollis Brown. That name sounds familiar."

After the earlier discussion about Dylan's music, Frank was confounded that his dogmatic passenger had a fake ID with the name of that tragic person immortalized by the North Country bard's song.

This was taking longer than necessary, Frank thought. And it was becoming even more fraught.

"How about you two showing me your draft cards?"

Jesus H. Christ thought the frightened driver fleeing to Canada with another fugitive from justice.

Stammering, Frank was prepared to confess that neither had one since he was a draft resister and his passenger had burned his card. At the perilous moment, a big smile crossed the face of the Canadian official.

"Just joking with you guys. Welcome to Canada and good fishing."

With a deep sigh of relief, Frank took back the two driver's licenses. Wary of accelerating too fast, he hardly pushed down on the gas pedal. As the Corvair passed through Fort Frances, he saw the sign indicating the route to Thunder Bay. Turning in that direction, he looked forward to getting a quick bite there and then on to Toronto where he and the mysterious stranger would become anonymous city dwellers with their own secret past lives.

Twenty-Two

MID-DECEMBER 1967

With the near completion of the 1967 Fall Quarter, Mary and Frank contemplated a road trip to Pittsburgh to meet his parents. They would have to stop in Chicago in order to break up the long drive and spare themselves the boredom of a whole day on the road. If it snowed on their way to or from Pittsburgh that tedium could morph into terror, especially with the notoriously "unsafe-at-any-speed" Corvair. As a hedge against the dangers inherent in any daylong drive, Frank called his cousin in Chicago and arranged with him to stay overnight on both legs of the journey.

The telephone conversation with his father about the prospective visit with a girlfriend in tow had followed predictable lines of inquiry about who this woman was. First and foremost, his dad asked whether she was Jewish. When Frank replied that she was a "fallen-away" Catholic, he could hear an audible guffaw on the other end. Then came the clincher of a question, "She isn't colored, is she?" Oh Gawd, thought Frank, is this my "Guess Who's Coming to Dinner" moment? Assuring his father that her "color" was "a whiter shade of pale" (an allusion to the Procol Harum tune his dad would never comprehend), Frank terminated the discussion by noting they would be in Pittsburgh within the week.

The only caveat that Mary brought up was the need to be back in Minneapolis to celebrate Christmas with her family. Fortunately for Frank, the observation of that most *goyish* of holidays (with the possible exception of Easter with its sado-masochistic story of crucifixion and fairy-tale ending of resurrection) would only require him to be present for the waffle dinner before Midnight Mass. Since he didn't have to attend any church service with the family, this did not seem like a very onerous commitment. Besides, he loved waffles. He could even regard the waffle as a substitute wafer for his communion with Mary's Irish-American family.

When the day arrived for their departure, the grey skies and blustery weather threatened a possible snowstorm. He hoped that driving east and south would avoid the winter sneak attack. To keep their spirits up on the drive to Chicago, Frank and Mary traded singing uplifting songs. First, he tried to sound like Jackie Wilson in his own rendition of "Higher and Higher," emphasizing for Mary's benefit that her love did lift him higher and higher. For her part, she attempted to imitate Marvin Gaye's distinctive intonations and Tammi Terrell's superb soprano in "Ain't No Mountain High Enough." Frank joined Mary in the chorus: "Ain't no mountain high enough/Ain't no valley low enough/Ain't no river wide enough/To keep me from getting to you babe." Their joyful styling of contemporary soulful sounds, if not accurate or authentic, carried them like a cosmic chariot into the Windy City.

Navigating the Corvair around Chicago's Near North Side, Frank was able to locate his cousin Harry's brick house. Parking the car was another matter since the street was solidly lined with bumper-to-bumper automobiles. Making Mary the lookout, he drove through several contiguous avenues while she cast an eagle eye for any possible breach in the chain of cars. They found a suitable opening only a few blocks away. After wedging the Corvair into the tight space, Frank and Mary retrieved their overnight bags from the trunk and circled back on foot to Harry's place.

Because it was the weekend, his cousin was home. Greeting them warmly after they rang his doorbell, he led them through the house to the little kitchen in the back.

"Would you like some lemonade or a beer?"

Frank chose the beer. Mary preferred the lemonade. Both happily relaxed with their libations in hand.

"Since it's Saturday night, I made reservations at a local Indian restaurant that's my favorite. It comes closest to what I remember eating on my trek to India."

Harry, the only son of Frank's Uncle Morty, spent a year traveling around the globe after living in Thailand where Morty had a Fulbright Fellowship. After finishing up his undergraduate degree at Indiana University where his dad taught in the Political Science Department, Harry had gone on to get his MSW (Master of Social Work) at the University of Chicago. He was now a social worker in the city, staving off the burnout that all too frequently affected those in a welfare bureaucracy contending with the institutional holes in the social safety net. Harry's dedication to eking out some modicum of justice and dignity for his clients was nevertheless punctuated by his common mantra, "We're losing the battle out there."

Tonight none of them would worry about the struggles on either the domestic or foreign fronts. Instead, Harry would regale them with wondrous tales of his worldly experiences while introducing both Frank and Mary to the delicacies of Indian cuisine.

From the breads stuffed with potatoes and onions to the wide variety of curries and finally to a dessert of warm rice pudding, they were satiated with the food and his cousin's stories. The beers they consumed along with the meal helped lull them into a deep sleep in the tiny bed they shared in the second floor extra bedroom.

When Frank and Mary awakened, the sun was just rising. Since Harry was still sound asleep, they quietly gathered their things and tiptoed down the stairs and out the front door. They would grab breakfast on the road after putting in an hour or two of driving. The food available in the franchise restaurants that dotted the interstate highways was a contrast in so many ways to their Indian repast last night. Where the spices and freshness had delighted their taste buds yesterday evening, the plastic bland-tasting fare offered for their morning and midday meals was an affront to those same taste buds.

Fortunately, there were no other assaults on their senses other than the monotony of the flat repetitive farmland abutting the Ohio Turnpike. Even their spirits became duller as they were reduced to playing alphabet word games. Once the more hilly parts of Western Pennsylvania appeared, Frank's mood changed. It was as if the undulating topography through which he now traversed soothed any and all edginess of the long trip and apprehension about the interactions with his parents.

Unlike the jammed urban neighborhood streets of Chicago, the suburb outside Pittsburgh where his parents resided offered plenty of parking, especially in the outsized concrete driveways that bordered the manicured lawns of each and every house. Pulling into the driveway now next to the Pontiac station wagon his dad still used for delivering lamps from his furniture store, Frank was overcome with trepidation. Although he assiduously avoided being drawn into any political arguments with his father, it was going to be difficult to sidestep discussing the repercussions of his draft resistance stance.

Maybe Mary's presence would provide a buffer to any conflicts that might arise during the next few days of their stay at his parents.

"Hey, mister," she chirped, "I need you to take the lead here."

He shook his head back and forth several times in order to get his bearings and prepare himself for his entrance into the family home, haunted, as it was, with the ghosts of past disputes and transgressions. Looking over at Mary's glowing face, he intended to rely on her radiance to cast out the darkness that might emerge from any negative encounters with his parents.

"Follow me," he gallantly declared as he forged forward. "I'll get our luggage later." The delay in transporting their bags may also have been a ploy by Frank to devise a back-up plan in case things got really unbearable for him and they needed to make a quick retreat to a hotel.

Because his mom had stationed herself for the last hour next to the large living room window that looked out on the street, she saw the Corvair, the car she had driven before giving it to her son, make the turn into the driveway. Rushing to the front door of the split-level house and calling out to her husband about the arrival of the young couple, Frank's mother eagerly waited to greet them. Catching sight of her, Frank bounded up the stairs, momentarily oblivious of his companion and lover. Retreating to take Mary's hand, he thrust her into his mother's arms.

"Mom, meet Mary," he announced. They embraced.

From behind he could hear his father complaining that he was being overlooked.

"I hear you dad. You're next."

Mary waited for Frank to hug his mom and then both proceeded to attend to his dad.

"So, this is the young lady who has enchanted my wayward son. Glad to make your acquaintance. Here's hoping you can put him on the straight-and-narrow."

"Well," Mary responded, "Your son does have a pretty strong will. I'm not sure how much influence I can wield."

"I'm confident that smile of yours can win a lot of arguments."

Mary's smile, indeed, was part of a charm offensive that won over Frank's parents almost immediately. For those several days in the Goodman household, her vivaciousness and warmth mitigated any of the tense arguments about the war and his Selective Service status. Still, he hesitated to reveal the full implications of his draft resistance during their stay with his parents. He promised himself that a long letter of explanation would be the more prudent tactic. So, they left without marring the obvious joy his parents felt at Mary's involvement with their son.

During the drive to Chicago, Frank was pensive. Pursing her lips in a way that indicated she was upset, Mary refrained from interrupting his silence. Instead, she fiddled with the radio, trying to locate stations playing the Top 40 hits. Whenever any Beatles song came on the air, his brooding stopped as he and Mary joined in to sing along, especially with the new release "All You Need is Love." The tuneful mantra of the chorus, repeating again and again, "all you need is love," helped dissipate any hint of despair that may have crept into his consciousness as a consequence of the realization of what his draft resistance would mean to his parents and to Mary, let alone to his future.

The overnight stop in Chicago at his cousin's also provided a wonderful respite from both conflicted thoughts and road weariness. Unfortunately, when they woke up the following morning, there was already an inch of snow on the ground. The Corvair only had a slight dusting on its windows, but as they drove north out of the city they encountered a blizzard. By the time they got to Madison, the roads were rather treacherous. So, Frank pulled into a rest stop to wait until the snow abated and he no longer had to contend with any whiteouts. Although the drive back to Minneapolis was hazardous, the Corvair managed to plow through the dangerous road conditions, dodging any accidents on the way.

By the time they arrived back at the West Bank home in Minneapolis, they were exhausted. Trudging into a cold house, Mary turned on the space heater while Frank retrieved the mail from the last few days of their absence. In the pile was the letter he was dreading from the Selective Service System. As he opened it, he tried to inject some levity into the fraught situation by singing another Beatles song: "I got the news today, oh boy. About a lucky man who…."

Before he could finish, Mary cut short his attempt to make light of what they both knew would be a possible rupture in their lives.

"Is that your notice?" She repeated her question with all the clarity that she amplified so exquisitely, "Is that your notice to report for induction?"

"Yes, ma'am. My Uncle Sam really rushed this along. It's been a little over two months since I sent in my draft card and wham-bam-thank-you-Sam, here's my official notice that I, Franklin Roosevelt Goodman, am now 1A and ordered to report to induction on January 15, 1968. I wonder if any other guys from TCDAC got their notices?"

"I don't care about the others, Frank. What are we going to do?"

"Mary, we've gone over this time and time again. Do I have to rehash my rationale. I'm obviously never going to convince you about publicly refusing induction and then facing the legal consequences. This is the only way to put my body on the line and gum up the gears of the war machine."

"That rhetoric is so smug and self-righteous that it's downright suffocating. If this country doesn't choke you to death, then you'll do it all by yourself. For what?"

"Somebody has to stand up to the system. This kind of action will shock people into a recognition of the insanity of the war while galvanizing even more efforts of resistance."

Frank said these lines almost automatically. His discourse was as predictably sloganeering as the antiwar buttons he wore on his clothes.

Waving aside these points, Mary reiterated her concern. "I don't want to hang around while you martyr yourself. Please, let's go to Canada. I have landed immigrant status and you'll find something to do. This country doesn't deserve any more martyrs."

It would take about two and a half years for Frank to accept the logic of Mary's position on going to Canada. In the interim, much would transpire, including their breakup, her desire to complete her Ph.D., and his fugitive status.

Surprising himself, Frank asked her, "Will you marry me?"

Taken aback, Mary pondered the abrupt change in the conversation and his proposal.

"Are you serious? We're still getting to know one another. I'm not sure it makes any sense to rush into this."

His upbeat response was once more to rely on the Beatles refrain: "All you need is love…"

"Can we wait until after Christmas and then discuss what this would mean?"

"Sure, but remember, 'love is all you need.'" Although he sang this with conviction, Frank had his doubts.

Twenty-Three

DECEMBER 24-25, 1967

Christmas eve found Frank with Mary's family, sitting around the dinner table. Her burly crew-cut dad, a supervisor for the local electric company, was ill at ease with this lanky long-haired stranger accompanying his only daughter to the ritual meal they consumed before attending midnight mass. Mary's mom, a dainty and dour Irish middle-aged woman, dutifully served the waffles and sausages to those gathered in her dining room. Along with her husband, she suspiciously eyed her daughter's boyfriend, especially after Frank admitted that he had never celebrated Christmas because he was Jewish. Her two sons, the older, a spitting image of his father, attended Mankato State University, and the younger, resembling the body type of his mother with a contrasting happy disposition, was a high school student.

Very little was said beyond the brothers asking for seconds. Frank certainly did not wish to begin any conversation for fear that a misplaced political reference by him might cause immediate strife and later indigestion. Only when the younger brother asked him about his future plans did he feel the need to prevaricate and mumble something about teaching high school. This mealy-mouthed response, nonetheless, encouraged Mary's youngest brother to follow up with a series of questions about what subject he wanted to teach (history) and what grades (juniors and seniors). After this exchange had exhausted the limits of conversation, the father announced that it was time to leave for church. Mary had indicated earlier that she and Frank would not be going with the rest of the family to midnight mass. So, after her apologies and his appreciation for the meal, they excused themselves and left.

When they arrived back at their West Bank abode, Mary hurried into the house. Earlier in the day she had convinced Frank that they needed a Christmas tree for celebrating the season and decorating the rather decrepit-looking living room. He had only offered a tepid objection, based on the fear that a dried-out tree, anywhere near the space heater, might catch on fire. She promised to keep it watered and to get rid of it once it started to lose its needles. As a concession to his concerns, she only strung a few simple white lights around the tree. Once those were turned on, even Frank had to admit it brightened the living room.

While he was staring at the tree, Mary hauled out a large sleeping bag and unfurled it next to the lit Christmas greenery.

"What's that for?" queried Frank.

"For us. We're going to sleep next to the tree tonight."

He was hesitant to argue with her, especially after she peeled off all of her clothes and stood naked before him. Against the backdrop of the white lights, Mary's curvaceous body was like a sensual adornment that beckoned him to indulge in some holiday cheer. He quickly undressed. They wrapped themselves in the sleeping bag, careful not to roll onto the tree during their physical exertions.

Frank awoke first. The decorative lights still shone even as sunshine was illuminating other corners in the house. He delicately extracted himself from the sleeping bag and quietly sought out his backpack where he had deposited the gift for Mary. Retrieving the small box, Frank opened it to check on the item he purchased as a holiday surprise for her. He sat down and waited until she opened her eyes. When she did, he knelt down next to her.

"What's in the box," she yawned.

"A gift for you."

"Let me get yours so we can open them together."

"No, first look what's inside for you."

Mary lifted the lid. The gold band gleamed brightly. Since she was transfixed, he took it out of the box and slipped it on her ring finger where it snugly fit. Then, he asked the question once more.

"Mary, will you marry me?"

Crying softly, she nodded her assent. He wrapped her in his arms as if she were the most perfect present he could imagine. He had been prepared to argue his case for matrimony as a necessary bonding to guarantee her legal right to visit him during his anticipated incarceration for violating the draft laws. She negated that need with her quick consent.

"Where did you get this ring?"

"Fred Adamson's uncle, Barry, is a jeweler. I picked it up the other day from Fred at the TCDAC office."

"Maybe I should return the gift I got you, a briefcase, and buy you a ring."

"Not necessary. Let's just figure out how we're going to put together a wedding in the next few weeks before I refuse induction. So, are there any judges who are antiwar who could do the marriage ceremony?

"Don't think so. How about the Unitarian minister? I know he and his congregation are against the war since they have a "Stop the War" sign outside the church. I'll call him up tomorrow and arrange a meeting."

The church, more correctly designated as the Unitarian "society" to distinguish it from doctrinaire religious establishment edifices, was located in downtown Minneapolis not far from the famous Walker Art Center. The minister was a former rabbi who, like other dropout Jews, converted to an idiosyncratic spiritual practice that was both liberal and eclectic. During their conversation with him, he regaled them with stories about his prior life and present predicament in conducting services that were inclusive enough to satisfy his disparate congregants. He was not offended when Frank requested that there be no references during the marriage ceremony to the Imaginary Friend in the sky. Not only was the minister extremely accommodating, but once he found out that Frank was a draft resister he insisted that all expenses be waived, adding that their organist would also play for free.

Having settled on a mutually agreeable day and time for the wedding, Frank and Mary began the process of inviting a limited number of friends to the celebration. Many of the invitees were incredulous that they were getting married so quickly until they were told about why it was being done so expeditiously. Some of the prospective guests were already scheduled to be at the Unitarian Society that same day for a meeting of Eugene McCarthy organizers in the building's basement. So, the reception was arranged to make sure those few folks would have the opportunity to celebrate with the happy couple. Frank's parents were informed and expressed their regrets. Mary's parents refused to come because the marriage was outside the Catholic Church. So, no relatives attended.

The wedding day dawned as one of the coldest mornings of the notoriously frigid Minnesota winters. The Corvair wouldn't start. Fortunately, Vince and Bonnie's car was a more reliable vehicle for these freezing temperatures. The warmth generated by the ceremony, punctuated as it was by the magnificent, if somewhat eccentric, organ performance of the Shaker Hymn, "Simple Gifts," and then the Beatles, "All You Need is Love," more than compensated for the wintry weather. The reception was further enlivened by the whole McCarthy crew from the basement below joining in with the revelry above. Given the cold climate outside and the political atmosphere surrounding the month of January 1968, a month that would end with a major shock to the U.S. war effort in Vietnam, this momentary celebration of love was a joyful reprieve.

Twenty-Four

EARLY FEBRUARY 1995

The reprieve hadn't lasted long – only six months. That was the time between the diagnosis and radiation treatment of her mother's breast cancer and her death by the invasive tumors that spread throughout her lymph nodes. Although Ruth knew that breast cancer could be particularly lethal to someone as young as her mother, dying at the age of forty-nine seemed so cruel. A hastily called memorial for her mom, Mary Browne, at the First Unitarian Universalist Church of Detroit, brought together many of her colleagues from Wayne State University, long-time friends in the area and from Minneapolis, and her two brothers and their families. Now that they all had departed, Ruth was left sorting through the belongings at the house in which she grew up, a house that Mary bought when she began her career in 1975 as an Assistant Professor in the English Department at Wayne State.

Although her mother had never married, she shared a three bedroom Dutch colonial with Ernie Bender from 1976 until his tragic death in 1984. He had gone to Nicaragua that year with Witness for Peace to work in rural villages, helping to set up clean water systems. In one of those remote villages on the border between Lake Nicaragua and Costa Rica, he had been captured and then killed by the Contras, the thuggish anti-Sandinista paramilitary forces, aided by the Reagan Administration, who terrorized the countryside. During the time Ernie lived with Mary, he became Ruth's surrogate father. Whether it was driving her to piano or kickboxing lessons or arranging elaborate birthday celebrations, he demonstrated his loving care for her.

As far as her birth father, her mom revealed little or next to nothing about him. Mary told Ruth that the affair was a desperate attempt at intimacy during a tumultuous time when she was a graduate student at the University of Minnesota. According to her mother, he didn't even know that he had impregnated Mary. Once he left Minneapolis for Canada, she had lost all contact with him and he never bothered trying to reach out to her.

So, for Ruth, this was a mysterious stranger. In deference to her mom, she resisted any inclination to find out what had happened to him. With the passing of her mother, there might be the time and space to investigate his whereabouts and something of his life.

Perhaps, the two lockboxes Ruth retrieved from her mom's clothes closet might hold a clue or two about her birth father. Opening the first metal container, Ruth found a mix of photographs, letters, and other memorabilia mostly from her childhood. One of the earliest photos was of Ruth promenading during *Carnivale* in Venice on the *Riva Degli Schiavone* with a blue balloon gripped tightly in her little hand. Her mother had a Fulbright to teach nineteenth-century American literature as Junior Fellow in the Anglo-American Studies program at the University of Venice. Because she was so young, a mere three-year-old when they arrived from their lengthy trip by plane and train to that watery wonderland, so many of her memories were hazy except for those that Mary reinforced by her story-telling of their adventures in Italy. Another photograph, dated on the back from 1977, was of her on Ernie's shoulders at the Detroit Zoo Penguinarium.

Mary had saved a number of certificates that had marked certain passages in Ruth's childhood. Among them were the graduation certificates from Taft Elementary School and Best Middle School. Her special Honor degrees from Ferndale High School and the University of Michigan were also in the mix. Ruth discovered the award letter she had received as winner of the Mozart piano competition at Blue Lake Music Camp. Tucked in among these certificates and notifications was the court document from Washtenaw County for the assault charge against a police officer during a 1990 abortion clinic defense. Ruth found the letter she had written her mom about that arrest and why she had been unfairly charged since it was the cop who assaulted her first. The charge probably resulted from what happened when she applied her kickboxing training and knocked the cop on his ass. Of course, Mary had bailed out her daughter, but the ensuing discussion had turned into an awful argument that left both a little hurt. Hence, the apologetic tone of the letter.

Another letter, not at all apologetic, was the five-page single-spaced missive that Ruth felt compelled to write after her junior year at the University of Michigan. It was her "coming out" *cri de coeur,* a passionate revelation of the personal and political reasons for her sexual orientation as a gay woman. As she skimmed the contents of the letter, certain passages captured her attention. She smiled when she read through the reference to her first infatuation with someone of her own sex, a skateboarding, Goth-attired high school classmate. Several pages were devoted to the impact of the class she had audited in college with Catherine McKinnon where she encountered for the first time the works of Andrea Dworkin. Although, as she explained in her letter, unconvinced of their perspectives on pornography, Ruth fully accepted how McKinnon and Dworkin criticized a male supremacist social order that subordinated and exploited women, committing violence against the "second" sex whether in intimate or legal relationships. Reflecting on these passages, in particular, she more fully understood the motivation for becoming a director of a women's shelter after graduating from Michigan.

Returning that letter and all the other materials to the metal container, Ruth pulled the other lockbox toward her. For this one she needed a specially marked key that she found in the bottom drawer of her mom's old wooden desk. When she opened the box, she saw that it was stuffed with a variety of legal documents, including an additional copy of Mary's will and the deed to their house. Buried beneath these ponderous papers was a sealed envelope with a slight protuberance. Carefully tearing open the envelope, she extracted a ring, a simple gold band which she set aside as she turned her attention to the enclosed paper. Ruth unfolded a document listed as a Hennepin County marriage certificate. Her shock was mitigated by a curious scrutiny with which she examined it. There was both a date, January 6, 1968 and a name, Franklin Roosevelt Goodman, attached to the document. Why her mother lied about and covered up this marriage was a conversation that Ruth would not be able to conduct. She would, however, make an effort to track down that person now revealed as her birth father.

Twenty-Five

JANUARY 15, 1968

Franklin Roosevelt Goodman received official marching orders from the Selective Service System wrapped in a bundle of bureaucratic paperwork. As a consequence of returning his draft card to the local board in Pittsburgh where he was registered, he had to request a transfer to report for induction in Minneapolis. The brief letter he sent, dated December 28, 1967, to Local Board No. 10, declared the impossibility of returning to Pittsburgh on January 15, the date of the induction notice, because of his residence in Minneapolis and his forthcoming wedding, not to mention his student status at the University of Minnesota, a status the he had renounced in his prior communication. Included with the letter was the first and only Selective Service official document he signed.

When the "Order for Transferred Man to Report for Induction" arrived in the mailbox at the West Bank home address, it listed the same date as the original, January 15, but with specific instructions as to time, 6:30 A.M., and place, Second Floor Lobby of the Federal Office Building on 3rd and

Washington in downtown Minneapolis. Accompanying this document was a raft of official paperwork, all of which he ignored. Instead of filling out DD Form 398, "Statement of Personal History," with its extensive questions about employment, education, residences, and credit and character references, Frank, marching to the beat of his own drummer, composed a flyer, which he distributed to those sleepy-eyed and nervous inductees on the freezing morning of January 15. The propagandistic protest leaflet was addressed to his "Brothers" and read as follows:

Today, we will face either pre-induction physicals or actual induction into the army. Each of us brings our own perspectives and principles to this induction center. I am a graduate student at the University of Minnesota. I could have had a deferment, but I refused to accept preferential treatment. I returned my draft card to my local board in October as a personal means of protest against the policies of conscription and war. I felt that the Selective Service System was immoral and illegal because of its inequities and infringements upon an individual's conscience.

I believe that the war in Vietnam is immoral and illegal because of the killing of innocent Vietnamese and the disregard our government has shown towards international treaties, like the United Nations Charter and the Geneva Accords. Furthermore, Congress never declared war. LBJ is prosecuting an unjust and unpopular war in the greedy interest of the military-industrial complex. At the outset of the military escalation in 1964, President Johnson said: 'We don't want to send American boys over there to do the job that Asian boys should do for themselves.' Now, in 1968, over 16,000 American soldiers have died for the selfish interests of the policy-makers who sit in their comfortable offices and send more guys to their deaths.

The people, you and I included, have not had the freedom of choice to decide on the question of the war after being presented with all of the true facts.

Today, our freedom of choice is again being denied. Even if some of you want to fight, you may have been forced to make that decision because of economic hardships that were caused by the diversion of funds to carry on a costly war. There will be a demand made on you by the military to sign a security questionnaire without presenting to you a complete picture of your rights. However, under the Fifth Amendment of the United States Constitution, you need not fill out the form. Your private life and beliefs are your own business. To let your privacy and principles be traduced without total awareness of those rights is to give up your claim to manhood.

DON'T LET YOURSELF BE REDUCED TO A SLAVE!

Don't blindly follow the dictates of others without probing your own conscience for your true convictions. The government and the army have to fully explain themselves to you about their policies before they can make exorbitant demands on your life. Assert your manhood by demanding the rights guaranteed to you under the Constitution and in conjunction with the principles of common humanity. Ask any pertinent questions to reveal the true facts. But, most of all, consult your conscience and do what you feel is just and consistent with the precepts upon which this country was founded:

LIFE, LIBERTY, AND THE PURSUIT OF HAPPINESS!

Smugly believing that his conscience-stricken and compelling arguments would sway at least a few of the potential inductees, Frank was taken aback when the handing out of the flyer was met with indifference and, in one instance, with overt hostility. Nonetheless, he trailed the line of scared young men up to the Second Floor Lobby where they were told to wait to be called for their physicals. Some had already entered the room where the physical examination was being conducted. He could hear a minor commotion from inside the room. This provided ample opportunity to begin his harangue. Reiterating many of the points raised in the flyer, Frank appealed to his cohorts to deny the military their bodies before they were turned into cannon fodder for a malignant war-machine. Before he could start a more esoteric rant that echoed the denunciations of "Moloch" in Allen Ginsberg's poem, "Howl," he was yanked from the lobby by two MP's and deposited on a wooden chair across from a large desk in an empty office.

In addition to the door that opened to the lobby through which Frank was hustled, there was a separate access to the physical examining room. He could hear some tussling directly behind that entrance. The door swung open and an army officer, impeccably dressed with several brightly-colored medals adorning his drab olive uniform, swept into the office, followed by another stern looking army automaton of lower rank. As the officer seated himself behind the desk, the other military man, gripping a nearly naked civilian by both arms, shoved this trembling figure onto the adjacent chair. Frank was startled to see that the guy next to him, clad only in white underpants, was a denizen of the West Bank known only as JJ. One of the few neighbors who wasn't a student, JJ was an auto mechanic, but also a fervent antiwar activist who, upon hearing that Frank was a draft resister, presented him with a piece of lumber upon which he carved a prosaic diatribe against the draft. The common refrain on the wooden memento was "Fuck the Draft, Fuck the Draft, Take it up the Ass, you fuckin draft."

JJ was also surprised to see Frank sitting next to him, but managed to whisper in a low co-conspiratorial voice that he had found his own way to beat the draft. At this point, the ramrod stiff officer, looking straight at JJ, scowled and barked out a seemingly ludicrous question, "Why do you have peanut butter up your ass?"

JJ smiled and replied, "That's where I keep it to make my peanut butter and jelly sandwiches."

Incredulous, the sputtering army lieutenant launched his own rather unprofessional tirade against JJ, "Listen, you candy-assed pervert, I know this is just a ruse to get out of the military. If I could, I'd take that peanut butter and jam it down your throat."

Smacking his lips, JJ responded with a yummy sound.

"Okay, mister, you're out of here with the 4F you were obviously seeking with this little ruse of yours."

Dragged from the chair by the other disgusted and red-faced member of the military, JJ disappeared into the exam room from whence he came.

Turning now to Frank, the officer was perusing the flyer that had been put on his desk.

In a mocking tone, the lieutenant exclaimed, "So, it's your little conscience that is bothering you? Well, maybe you'll have more time to think about this drivel you wrote from inside a prison where I expect you'll be languishing for the next five years."

As the officer stood up, so did Frank.

"I want you out of here this minute."

Calling in one of the military men that had pulled Frank into the office, the army officer gave an order to "Get this reprobate out of here. And take him down the backstairs so his buddies on the outside won't have a chance to cheer this lousy traitor."

The door slammed shut. Frank had no intention of following the orders that the army subordinate was compelled to obey. Turning on his heel, Frank scurried down the hall and steps towards the front entrance of the Federal Building. Outside in the bitterly cold weather were gathered his comrades from the TCDAC, other friends and antiwar activists. Mary, his wife of one week, rushed over to embrace him as the crowd started to sing the old civil rights hymn, "Ain't Gonna Let Nobody Turn Me Around." Some actors from the Firehouse Theater began performing an excerpt from Megan Terry's musical, "Viet Rock." As one of their female members disrobed, all huddled closer together for both warmth and comradeship. The drama soon ended.

Twenty-Six

Several dramas, public and private, were unfolding in the nation's capital and in Vietnam during the latter half of January 1968 that would have profound implications for Washington's war effort in Southeast Asia. On that exact date, January 15, as Frank was refusing induction in Minneapolis, 5000 women, under the banner of the "Jeannette Rankin Brigade," marched on Capitol Hill. Rankin had been a congressional representative from Montana during World War I and World War II, voting against the declaration of war in both instances. Assembled by the pacifist organization, Women Strike for Peace (WSP), the black-clad female demonstrators were denied entrance to the Capitol Building, presumably because the overwhelmingly male congressional representatives perceived the protestors as harassing harpies.

Almost nine thousand miles away, on the South Vietnam border with Laos in the region known as the "Demilitarized Zone" (DMZ), the U.S. Marine base at Khe Sanh came under attack from several divisions of the North Vietnamese Army

(NVA). The battle, initiated by artillery strikes from the NVA on January 21, 1968, unleashed massive amounts of ordnance from both sides. The total U.S. aerial bombardment during the months-long siege was around 100,000 tons.

While the Pentagon and White House were concentrated on defeating the enemy at Khe Sanh, the diversion allowed the National Liberation Front to build up its forces all across South Vietnam. On January 31, the Tet New Year, a vast surprise attack reached into every urban area in South Vietnam, including the U. S. military headquarters and Embassy in Saigon. While the Tet Offensive resulted in heavy losses for the NLF, the public fantasies promulgated by the Pentagon and the White House of a "great victory" could not suppress the realization that Washington had not won the "hearts and minds" of the Vietnamese and there was not, as so often promoted by the Johnson Administration and its supporters, "a light at the end of the tunnel." In private meetings behind closed doors in the corridors of power in D.C., the assessment of the war effort after Tet led to sobering conclusions. Dissident whispers about the collapsing situation in Vietnam among Washington policy-makers were amplified in the news reports in the *New York Times* and *Washington Post*. There were even suggestions that the reason for the resignation of Secretary of Defense Robert McNamara at the end of February was because he and some of his staff sensed that the Vietnam war could not be won.

During the winter of 1968, President Johnson confronted growing discontent within his party and in the nation at large. Public opinion was turning against the war even as some in the media, like the avuncular television journalist Walter Cronkite, actually began to question the Johnson

Administration's rationale and claims for the war effort. When the laconic Senator Eugene McCarthy of Minnesota challenged LBJ in the Democratic primaries, shocking him and the nation with over forty percent of the vote in New Hampshire, it led to Senator Robert Kennedy's entrance into the presidential race. Seeing the writing on the wall, not wanting to suffer any more political humiliation, and worried about his health, LBJ then surprised the nation with his announcement on March 31, 1968 that he "would not seek (and) not accept the nomination...for another term as President."

The shouts of joy in response to this news echoed around the frigid streets of Minneapolis and throughout all of the antiwar American enclaves. Frank and Mary tore out the door of their West Bank home and swept into the neighborhood hangouts, crying out that their constant protesting refrains of "Hey, Hey, LBJ, How many kids did you kill today?" had driven this hated President out of office. The elation was still evident three days later when thousands marched in Minneapolis and around the country for another draft card turn-in. Then, even more hit the streets for the massive rallies at the end of April sponsored by the new organization calling itself the "Moratorium."

It seemed to Frank that the tide was turning in favor of those opposed to the Vietnam War. Yet, at the same time, he could not quite see that he and his fellow militant draft resisters and antiwar protestors were becoming not only greater targets of repression by the government but also stereotyped symbols of the "wrong" kind of dissent. The alternate universe that he and his fellow activists inhabited would be unhinged by a series of events that started in April and concluded in August of 1968.

Twenty-Seven

APRIL 4-5, 1968

In the midst of the political upheavals in the early spring of 1968, Frank and Mary were also busy with their graduate work in American Studies. Even though the FBI had pursued Frank for his violation of the Selective Service Act, his lawyer, Chuck Truvold, had helped expedite the arrest, bail, and coming trial without much disruption in their lives. Both were occupied during the Spring Quarter as Teaching Assistants. Frank's Introductory Course in American Studies for undergraduate students focused on "Violence in American Life." Among the books they were reading was the 1932 classic, *Black Elk Speaks* about an Oglala Lakota shaman who survived the 1890 Wounded Knee Massacre. The class discussion of the book was scheduled for Friday morning April 5. Frank cancelled the session.

The night before on April 4, Dr. Martin Luther King, Jr. was assassinated in Memphis where he had gone to lend his support to the city's sanitation workers who were on strike. Frank had heard the late night news that evening about Dr.

King's murder and the explosions that rocked urban areas around the country. Although the response in the inner city sections of Minneapolis was relatively subdued, he completely sympathized with those who took to the streets elsewhere and engaged in what the media called "rioting." For Frank, these expressions of rage were justified even if they contradicted MLK's commitment to nonviolence.

During the intense period of his own involvement with the civil rights movement in Pittsburgh, he had been fortunate to meet Dr. King. In fact, he had introduced him when he visited the Pitt campus in the fall of 1966. After the talk, he and a select interracial group of students had lunch with the civil rights icon. Since Frank was sitting close to Dr. King at the meal, he ventured a question that was on his mind. He was positive that this movement leader would be able to answer it since it involved the issue of violence and nonviolence. Citing the large number of Black GIs fighting in Vietnam, Frank wondered how they could be converted to nonviolence. All he could recall from Dr. King's response was that it was a difficult matter to address in the little time left at the luncheon.

As Frank watched the television airing of images of flames engulfing buildings in city after city, the question he posed back in 1966 troubled his own mind now. In the face of the violence perpetrated by the system and its adherents against those deemed to be "threats" to that system, how could one expect the victims not to lash out, especially when those advocating nonviolence, like MLK, were, themselves, the victims of violence? All of these contradictions confounded Frank, unsettling his convictions. Mary tried to proffer solace, but he could find little comfort in her offer. And so, he hardly slept.

The next morning, having cancelled class, Frank went to the TCDAC office. When he arrived, Dan was already busy with mimeographing a flyer that contained passages from Dr. King's famous 1967 Riverside Church address where he denounced the Vietnam War, a denunciation that alienated many high-profile liberals. Picking up one of the leaflets, Frank was once again mesmerized by how incisive MLK's criticisms of the war were. Maybe that was why Dan was so intent on producing a flyer that reminded people of Dr. King's antiwar perspectives, especially in the aftermath of the assassination.

"How are you doing, Dan?"

"Just trying to process the tragedy and keeping churning out our antiwar and anti-draft materials. I need to re-supply our stock of paper. Can you hang out at the office for the rest of the morning?"

"Sure."

"Either Jim or Fred will be here around noon. Also, I should be back around that time."

Frank had planned on staying for a few hours, doing whatever mundane tasks were essential as a follow-up to the recent draft card turn-in. So, he didn't mind sticking around until being relieved by one of the other fellows.

About an hour after Dan left, two Black men sauntered into the office. The older more rugged one approached Frank and held out his hand.

"My name's Jamal Rice. This is my younger brother, Lamar. He's about to turn eighteen and I don't want him going to no damn Nam. I just got back from there and no self-respecting Blood should be fighting in that racist war. I should have followed Muhammad Ali's example and refused to be

160

drafted, but I didn't have his religious beliefs or his political conscience and courage. Now, I understand what he meant when he said 'No Viet Cong ever called me Nigger.'"

Still grasping Jamal's hand, Frank was overwhelmed by the righteous anger that this Vietnam veteran exuded. Vets like Jamal were just beginning to form antiwar organizations around the country, particularly in the form of coffee houses near military bases. He and his comrades at TCDAC had made contact with some VVAW (Vietnam Veterans Against the War) guys in the Twin Cities to find ways to work together. Now, here was an opportunity to be of some service and establish a link with a Black Vietnam Vet.

He directed Jamal and Lamar to move to the couch while he gathered up a variety of materials for Lamar to look over later.

"Here's some literature on applying for conscientious objector status, Lamar. Do you think that's something you might want to consider?"

Before Lamar could answer, Jamal intervened. "Look, there's no way he's gonna convince his white- dominated draft board that he's that kinda person. Maybe he should just leave and go to Canada. Probably fewer racists up there. Hell, there were a bunch of crackers in my outfit in Nam. Almost had a minor race war until our CO engineered a truce along with getting rid of the white racist sergeant. We almost fragged that bastard."

Frank had heard about some isolated incidents in Vietnam where young drafted grunts, in particular, killed an officer instead of obeying an order that increased the probability of their own deaths. Jamal now provided some anecdotal grounding to those stories of revenge and resistance within the military. Although intrigued by Jamal's experiences in the war, he had to turn his attention to Lamar.

"So, Lamar, what's your thinking about the draft and the war?"

Lamar hesitated for a minute and then stammered, "Don't wanna go. Ain't gonna fight."

Recognizing the anger and alienation embedded in those two short statements, Frank contemplated how to guide the conversation towards some more tangible intent.

"I understand, but if you register when you turn eighteen for the draft, they'll make you eligible for induction unless you're a student and you get a student deferment."

"Well, I'm thinkin about goin to the Minneapolis Community College. Does that count for a student deferment?

"Absolutely. You just need to keep up your grade point average. Do you plan on continuing after the two years at the community college?"

"Hopefully."

"Yeh, and hopefully the war will be over by then," Frank said without much confidence.

Jamal added his own twist to the prognosis for the war's end, "Just a quagmire over there. Anyhow, we've gotta fight the power over here. Maybe join up with that new organization, the Black Panther Party. Turn our weapon training to good use for finally gettin our freedom."

Frank had no words of advice to offer either Jamal or Lamar on this account. Remembering, again, the unanswered question about violence and nonviolence that he had posed to Dr. King, he just kept silent.

It was Lamar who broke that silence. "Thanks for all this literature. I guess I got some homework outta this."

"Yeh," said Frank, waking from his stupor. "Just call or come in if you've got any more questions."

As the two rose to leave, Jamal looked squarely into Frank's face and asked, "Why in the hell did they murder Dr. King? I mean the man was nonviolent and that's what he gets for all his efforts? So, where do we go from here?"

"I can't answer that for you. I know Dr. King wrote a book with that last question in the title. Maybe, there's an answer in there."

"Not sure words are what matters now," Jamal said, once again offering his hand to Frank.

"Good luck to both of you. Please keep in touch."

Walking out the door, into a daylight smudged by still smoldering stores in so many cities around the country, the two men, one battle-tested in Vietnam and the other wanting to avoid the fray, left Frank brooding over the paradoxes they and so many other people of color posed to a seemingly intransigent white power structure.

His meditative mood was interrupted when Jim Penny lumbered into the office.

His near permanent scowl now deepened by the events of last night, he just shook his head at Frank.

"Where's Dan?"

"Off getting more supplies."

"Did Fred stop by yet?"

"No, but Dan mentioned that both of you might show up around noon. Do you want me to stick around in case we want to meet and discuss the situation?"

"What situation? It's the same mess, just with one more senseless murder of an unarmed Black man. He just happened to be too prominent for his death to pass unnoticed. Maybe the fires this time will wake up the sleeping conscience of this nation.”

“I guess we can always hope.”

“The hell with hope. We’ve got to ring the alarms and add to the clamor for real change.”

For all his seeming sluggishness, Jim could, on occasion, arouse himself and those around him to some higher purpose. This moment of inspiration was brief and soon overcome by returning to the grind of more mundane matters. Frank decided to let Jim carry on without him. Saying farewell, he left the office and headed home.

When Frank arrived at the West Bank house and paused to get his key, he thought he heard Mary sobbing inside. As soon as he entered, she tried to pretend that she had not been crying and hid her face from him.

“What’s wrong?”

Without turning to look at Frank, she muttered something he couldn’t quite understand.

“Can you please repeat what you said so I can hear you?”

“I got my period.”

“So, it’s that time of the month, but why are you so emotional?”

“I didn’t have my period last month and I was hoping I was pregnant.”

Startled by her admission, he didn’t know how to respond at first.

“We didn’t even discuss this. Why would you want to get pregnant knowing I might have to go to prison and leave you alone with a child?”

Mary paused before answering. Considering her choice of words, she uttered, “I wanted a tangible bond of our love.”

"But this would have put an extra burden on you without me to help."

"I just felt I could handle this on my own."

He reached out to embrace her, adding soothing words about the strength of their love and other opportunities to get pregnant even as he stifled his longing of not wanting to bring a child into this world. But from now on, he promised himself to use condoms.

Twenty-Eight

LATE FEBRUARY 1995

"Have you told him that you're pregnant?"

"That selfish prick? He would kill me if he found out I was hiding this kind of secret from him. I thought maybe if I could wait for a more opportune time when he was less stressed out and appeal to his desire to be a father then he would welcome the idea and stop hurting me in the process."

Ruth recognized the wishful thinking inherent in these contradictory remarks. This particular upper middle class white woman, married to one of the lead prosecutors in Jackson County, tenaciously clung to the idea of having a baby as a way to mitigate or eliminate her husband's violent outbursts. Yet, her frequent appearances at S.A.V.E., the women's shelter in Jackson, hiding behind huge black Jackie O sunglasses that often covered her blackened eyes, were testimonies to the persistent viciousness of her patriarchal punisher. Terrified of alerting the police in order to press charges, this abused spouse, privileged as she was, cowered in fear of further retribution. Seeking a temporary retreat from her situation, she, nonetheless, returned to a household in the grip of a domestic terrorist.

As the Executive Director of S.A.V.E, Ruth Browne oversaw a staff of highly competent and committed women from the resident therapist, a brilliant Black Ph.D., to the dogged legal advisor, and other staff and volunteers. They all occupied offices on the third floor of a stately old mansion, donated by a wealthy woman whose inheritance allowed for such largesse. The other two floors contained the fifty beds used as an emergency shelter for both women and children fleeing from domestic or sexual violence. Overseeing the whole operation, including outreach to other county and state social services, Ruth was completing three years of challenging and rewarding work that enabled many of the women who sought refuge a new and better life where possible.

However, after three years and the death of her mother, Ruth was experiencing burnout. Her ability to "save" the women who came to this shelter from the systematic and institutionalized brutality they endured - first from their partners and then from a criminal justice system stacked against them - appeared more and more like a delusion. She did not look forward to another fall when, because of football season, the shelter would be overrun with women attempting to escape from the increased incidents of domestic violence that accompanied this brutal sport. When she read about a special graduate program in domestic violence in the Sociology Department of the University of Toronto, she had applied, not giving much thought to leaving her job and moving to Canada to pursue a doctoral degree. Now, feeling exhausted in her career and wanting a change of life, the inducement of the fellowship offered by the university pulled her in the direction of this new passage.

After telling the staff of her decision and investing the Assistant Director with all the authority she needed to carry out the various and weighty tasks of a director, she wistfully reflected on one of her last interactions with two clients, a Mexican-American mother and her young daughter. While the mom spoke to one of the Spanish-speaking counselors, Ruth took five-year-old Rosalie to the food pantry downstairs. The little girl spotted a brightly colored box with a highly sugared cereal, among the many such items donated by the Kellogg Corporation in nearby Battle Creek. Quickly, Ruth opened the cereal and poured it into a green plastic bowl that she handed to the happy youngster. Munching on the multi-colored little loops, Rosalie was led by Ruth to the clothes closet. Spotting a sparkly evening purse, the child longingly pointed to it as if it was precious plunder from some generous pirates. Ruth gladly bestowed this glittering gift on the wide-eyed kid and then accompanied her young charge back upstairs to join her mother.

Twenty-Nine

JANUARY TO AUGUST 28, 1968

His mother disjointedly completed Frank's call, repeating several times her goodbyes to him. The telephone conversation with his parents updated them on his prospective trial and probable prison sentence. Back in January when he last spoke to them about the quickly arranged marriage to Mary, he confessed that he had been reclassified 1-A after turning in his draft card in October. He explained why he would be refusing induction and talked about the possible repercussions. After his father listened carefully and without interrupting his son, there was a long pause on the line.

The silence was broken by a firm declaration from his dad. "Whatever you need, count on us. We're obviously concerned, but we support you."

"Thanks, Dad. That means so much to me. I'm just sorry you couldn't be here for the wedding. Hopefully, you can visit before I'm sent to prison."

"I hope it doesn't come to that. It would be such a waste."

"It's not a waste for me to stand up for fundamental principles."

"That may be so, but you're obviously not thinking about your future and Mary's."

"She and I both understand what this means for our life together. We're both prepared to handle this."

Although assuring his father of their resoluteness in this matter, Frank admitted to himself that there were very real tensions between Mary and him concerning the immediate and long-term prospects for their relationship and their lives. In any case, it was decided that the long Labor Day weekend would be a good time for a visit from his parents. Frank was plowing ahead with his course work in order to complete the degree requirements for his Master's in August before his dad and mom visited. That way they would have something to celebrate.

Celebrations were a rare occurrence for Frank, especially given the on-going slaughter in the jungles of Southeast Asia. While the episodic demonstrations provided a boost to the flagging optimism about stopping the war and ending the draft, there were rare surprise moments when a particularly audacious action elicited a spark of exaltation among the fellowship of draft resisters. One of those instances occurred on May 17, 1968 when two priests, Philip and Daniel Berrigan, and their seven Catholic comrades stormed into the Catonsville, Maryland local draft board and wrestled hundreds of 1-A files from the startled clerks. Once outside, the Catonsville Nine, as they would later be called in the trials that resulted in two- to three-year sentences, set the files on fire.

While a flame was certainly lit under the TCDAC crew, other antiwar activists saw the Catonsville Nine exploit as little more than militant moral witnessing. Among those who were dismissive of such actions was Vince Bourgeois, about to launch his legal career. He had become the titular head of the McCarthy campaign in the university area, inducting students into the "Clean-for-Gene" canvassing that followed the New Hampshire primary and preceded the Minnesota presidential caucuses in late May. Even Frank was somewhat seduced by McCarthy's antiwar speeches from that New Hampshire near victory. One of those talks that the Senator gave in the Granite State after Tet was reproduced in the flyer that was blanketing the West Bank and Cedar Riverside. It read in part:

In 1963, we were told that we were winning the war. In 1964, we were told we were winning the war. In 1965, we were told that the enemy was being brought to its knees. In 1966, in 1967, and now again in 1968, we hear the same hollow claims of programs and victory. The Democratic Party in 1964 promised "no wider war." Yet the war is getting wider every month. Only a few months ago we were told that 65 percent of the population was secure. Now we know that even the American Embassy is not secure.

While Frank was not ready to become a McCarthy convert, he certainly was prepared to participate in the Democratic caucus and cast a vote for the Senator. More germane, however, was the intention of the radicals in the neighborhood, which included Frank and Mary, to vote on the antiwar resolution they would offer at the caucus calling for an end to the war and an immediate withdrawal of U.S. troops from Southeast Asia. Mary had let Bonnie know about what would be proposed from the floor. She assured Mary that Vince would allow a discussion on the antiwar resolution and then a vote. Vince, however, had other plans. Once a decision was made about the presidential vote, Vince, as the Chair of the caucus, terminated the meeting with his McCarthy acolytes in tow.

Frank and Mary were outraged, but there was little they and their neighbors could do. Frank even considered getting involved in the Robert Kennedy campaign as a repudiation of the deceitful tactics of Vince and the so-called DFL reformers. Then, again, electoral politics was not the priority for him and what was now being referred to as "The Resistance." Yet, the night that Bobby Kennedy was assassinated after his June 4 win in the California primary provoked such sorrow and foreboding in Frank that for the rest of the week he found it difficult to leave the house. Once he did, the focus was on getting through all of the course requirements in the two summer terms.

While he never even considered going to Chicago in August for the planned demonstrations surrounding the Democratic Convention, a few of his more radical friends, including Bob Sagan, were anxious to remind the delegates, Mayor Daley and his minions, and the citizens of the city that there was still a war happening thousands of miles away. Little did they realize that the war would come home to the streets of Chicago and the protestors, McCarthy delegates, and innocent bystanders would experience what the blue ribbon commission that studied what transpired called a "police riot."

The stories that Frank and Mary heard from those, in particular, who were inside and outside the Hilton Hotel on the August 28 Wednesday evening the Chicago cops went berserk were truly terrifying. Bob Sagan was bludgeoned to the ground, left bleeding as the cop who wielded his baton as a weapon marched forward in a phalanx of menacing blue marauders screaming: "Kill, Kill, Kill." The Minnesota McCarthy campaigners, watching the melee from their windows above in the Hilton, were horrified by what they saw unfolding below. Soon, they also became the targets of police violence when Chicago cops busted down the door of the room in which they were gathered. When one of the lawyers in the group asked with visible exasperation on what legal grounds their room was illegally invaded, the lead cop responded with a smirk, "coffee grounds." Then, he and his fellow goons unleashed a torrent of blows on the unsuspecting victims.

And the bombs kept falling in Vietnam, expanding the number of victims in that war.

Thirty

With the Labor Day weekend over and his parents returning to Pittsburgh after their four-day visit, Frank looked forward to spending more time at the TCDAC office and working on antiwar and anti-draft activities. There were still a few papers that he had to submit for completion of his Master's degree. For the most part, however, his time on campus would be limited to coordinating with SASS and helping to build towards the next draft card return in November. As far as he was concerned, the election between Nixon and Humphrey seemed irrelevant to ending the war and the draft, irrespective of the campaign rhetoric delivered by either of the two presidential candidates. Doing politics for Frank meant staying away from the electoral circus, disregarding the shitting donkey and the stomping elephant, and organizing for confrontational mobilizations that challenged authority in all its various forms.

There were two other reasons why Frank could devote working hours to TCDAC. The combined savings that he and

Mary had accumulated with their teaching gigs would help them with expenses at least until the winter. In addition, Mary's assistantship in the English Department was continuing through the fall as she pressed forward with her course work for the doctorate. The other factor underlying Frank's decision to become a regular member of the TCDAC staff was the uncertainty of the outcome of his trial for violation of the Selective Service Act. Expecting a fall court date and then a waiting period for determining his sentence, he felt a little like the Saul Bellow character in *Dangling Man*, except in Frank's case he wasn't waiting to be inducted but to find out what refusing induction would mean for his future. So, to cite another Bellow book, he would *Seize the Day* and make the most of his life as he tried to live it in accordance with a sense of principled purpose.

Among his TCDAC comrades, Dan and Jim had also refused induction in late January. Now, the three of them were in legal limbo. Along with Fred and John, they were the stalwarts behind the draft resistance movement in the Twin Cities and the advocates for contesting the Selective Service System on college campuses, high schools, and religious communities throughout Minnesota or wherever else they were given a platform for their advocacy. As it turned out, an opportunity to open a branch office at Concordia College in Moorhead with access to Fargo, North Dakota, just across the Red River, brought all five of them to the office for a staff meeting in early September.

Opening the meeting with a review of recent counseling contacts, Dan solicited reflections on the tasks ahead.

Never shying away from taking the bull by the horns, so to speak, Jim jumped in with the opening salvo, "Well, I think I should be one of those going to Moorhead. I wouldn't want to stay there for any extended period. I'd probably make it a longer road trip and head further north and east to the Iron Range. Maybe I'd locate some pockets of resistance to mine up there."

Since Fred had made the initial contact at Concordia College, he felt compelled to put his hat in the ring. "I am prepared to spend as much time as possible, maybe six months or so, to do whatever it takes to confront the long arm of the Selective Service System in Moorhead. Even though my buddy, Stan, is not yet a draft resister, I think he is familiar enough with the ins and outs of the draft to accompany me on the journey."

Next, John Rider spoke up. "I wouldn't mind tagging along and then maybe heading up to the Iron Range with Jim. But I want to propose that we consider doing a more radical action as a Gang of Four when we get to Moorhead. You know that North Dakota has some of the most extensive missile sites in the country, all of them with nuclear warheads poised to blow the world to kingdom come. One of those sites, east of Fargo, is called Mt. Doom by some of the few anti-nuke activists in the state. We could coordinate with them for an action at the missile silo."

Expressing skepticism about the risks, Dan replied, "You're talking about trespassing on government property and risking arrest and jail time for a symbolic protest. That may be a waste."

John was quick to respond, "It's a greater waste that those missiles threaten our very existence. We need to arouse the public outrage and opposition needed to get rid of those demonic devices."

"I wouldn't mind taking an axe to one of those hellish weapons," Jim forcibly added.

Frank could see that John and Jim were getting caught up in their militant fantasies about attacking the Mt. Doom missile silo. Although he recognized the malevolent force that hovered over Mt. Doom and all the other nuclear missile sites, he feared that their collective rebellion was veering into the metaphysical instead of the historical. So, he sought to re-focus the discussion on the tasks for mounting a campaign in Moorhead.

"I think we need to keep on eye on the prize here and not wander off to taking on something that could end up destroying our efforts to build our movement."

Dan piped in, "I think Frank is right. We've got enough of an uphill battle without taking on destroying these missile bearers."

After a few more sputtering remarks about expanding the fight against the war machine, the five reached a consensus. Fred and Stan would set up an office in Moorhead, preferably at Concordia College where there might be more resources and help for their work. Jim and John would assist them in establishing their networks and then head out for the Iron Range. The four of them would leave from Minneapolis on September 23, leaving Dan and Frank to manage the TCDAC office with the periodic assistance from some student volunteers from SASS and Jim's sister, Eileen.

Once the four had left, Dan and Frank were kept busy with draft counseling. A few speaking engagements at local churches and colleges were shared by the duo as they spread the word about the November draft card turn-in. In the midst of this busy schedule and with the profile of TCDAC gaining more media attention, the office was set ablaze by parties unknown. While there was no structural damage, much of the literature was destroyed, leading both Frank and Dan to assume that there were government agents involved. Their belief was reinforced when the police showed little interest in pursuing any leads to catch those responsible for the fire.

In late October, right before Halloween, the federal spooks showed up to frighten Frank and Mary by bringing him to their show trial. If the charges of refusing to report for and submit to induction weren't so serious, the whole legal proceedings would have been a parody of a haunted house. The prosecuting attorney, a nervous rail-thin figure, like Ichabod Crane, fearful of his own shadow, constantly twirled rubber bands in his hands. Once when he approached the bench, one of those rubber bands shot up in the direction of the judge, a stern looking figure completely hidden in his large black robe. It almost decapitated the judge who, like some Headless Horseman, admonished the prosecuting attorney on his courtroom decorum. However, His Honor saved most of his wrath for Frank's attorney, Chuck Truvold. With a withering look towards Truvold, he browbeat the lawyer for the defense. Making clear his scorn for Frank, the silent ghost-like apparition in this courtroom stage show, the judge quickly dispensed the guilty verdict.

If the trial came off as a farce, the November 14 demonstration and draft card turn-in was hardly a tragedy. Indeed, the militant spirit of those who marched in the hundreds from campus to the Old Federal Building was palpable. Once the demonstrators arrived at their destination, several men stepped forward to either burn their draft cards or throw them on the ground in disgust. There was even a former vet who torched his discharge papers. In the midst of this rousing protest, Frank felt a certain disquietude about the future of such demonstrations and his own participation in these affairs.

Fortunately, for Frank and Mary the sentencing would get caught up in the slow moving bureaucracy of appeals and investigations, guaranteeing months and months of delay. During this time, Frank was out on bail without any particular restrictions on his movement or activities. So, he continued to work at the TCDAC office while Mary finished up the term with her course work and teaching assistantship.

Confronting another winter in that West Bank house with its single space-heater and a shower on the outside of the house motivated Frank and Mary to find somewhere else to live, especially a place that had more heat and a better shower. Mary's friend Marsha, who worked at Sovereign's Bookstore in the Cedar Riverside neighborhood, told her of the availability of the upstairs unit in a duplex she and her husband, Ted, rented near Powderhorn Park in South Minneapolis. After Frank and Mary inspected the apartment, noting the radiators in each room and the internal well-insulated shower, the prepared to move in before Christmas.

Realizing that he could no longer afford to work on the small salary he received at TCDAC, Frank started the search for a full-time regular decent paying job in December. That proved to be an ordeal. While checking out employment opportunities, Frank still spent a few days in the TCDAC office. One of the last young men he met there was Lamar Rice who, in more animated fashion this time, told him of his successful first term in community college, his student deferment, and his long-range plans to go to the "U." Like all such future aspirations, chance interventions could wreak havoc with even the best-laid plans. In Lamar's case, the cruel intrusion would be a more predictable extension of institutionalized white supremacy.

Thirty-One

DECEMBER 18, 1968 TO MAY 1969

The move into the duplex above Ted and Marsha went smoothly, especially since there was very little furniture and other belongings that Frank and Mary had to transport. Hiring a small van, they managed to shove all the larger items, like the worn-out couch, banged-up kitchen table, and wobbly old mattress, into the available space in the rented vehicle. Stuffing the Corvair with their clothes, record albums, record player, and their growing accumulation of books, they finished the relocation in one day, a week ahead of Christmas.

Ted and Marsha threw a welcoming party, inviting other neighbors from the Powderhorn area who shared the same movement politics and alternative life styles. Ted was a veritable one-man trip as Frank would learn over the next year. Having grown up in Minnesota, this blonde Swede embodied a Midwestern salt-of-the-earth personality with a heavy dose of hallucinogenic drugs that often transformed his blue eyes into what looked like a polluted particle of one of the ten thousand lakes said to dot the state's geography. Ted also combined a hippie sensibility with an odd mix of populism and Maoism. He was always trying to figure out how to swim, both literally and figuratively, in those bodies of water that would offer him both recreation and cover for his radical politics. Even though he tried to be wherever the action was, Ted often gave the impression of a wandering troubadour who upon entering one of those dense thickets in the North Woods, cried out: "Where the hell are we?"

If Ted's wanderings seemed, at times, almost Dantesque, then certainly his third wife, the voluptuous and virtuous Marsha Pinsker, did a good imitation of Beatrice. Marsha had her own marvelous personality: a dyed-in-the-wool Jungian whose Jewish earth-mother essence was too idiosyncratic to be stereotypical. While committed to converting all her friends and neighbors to healthy organic eating, she knew that alfalfa sprouts were not conducive to the Babeuf conspiracies being generated in her living room. Only blintzes could feed the soul of the displaced Easterners who found themselves arguing Talmudic points with Ted about the correct political line while debating the kinds of jam to spread on the blintzes and neglecting to consider Marsha's opinions unless it related to the toppings on her cheesy delights.

Mary had very little tolerance for those men who were dismissive of women's points of view. In fact, she often deliberately intervened in these heated discussions in the duplex down below with her own provocations. Frank was amazed at her *chutzpah*. Not that he exempted himself from the debates in Ted and Marsha's living room. Unlike Mary, however, he didn't feel the need to offer contrary perspectives even when they seemed appropriate to the conversation.

Nowhere was Mary's verbal combativeness more evident than at the New Year's Eve potluck at Ted and Marsha's, an occasion that would also be a surprise birthday celebration for Mary just after midnight on January 1, 1969. The object of her scorn was Al Himmelfarb who showed up at eleven o'clock, but left within the hour, perhaps as a consequence of Mary's righteous vitriol. Because Mary was familiar with the smug and arrogant Himmelfarb, having to tolerate his presence in a few of the American Studies grad courses, she was well primed for his haughty militant rhetoric.

The exchange between her and Himmelfarb started innocently enough when he waltzed into the party carrying his potluck contribution – a cherry pie. He announced this offering by paraphrasing H. Rap Brown, the former chairman of SNCC and sometime Black Panther: "I brought a cherry pie. Just as American as violence." Then he added the BP kicker: "Time to pick up the gun."

Mary leapt on that line. "You don't know which end of a gun to hold! Besides, it's pretty disingenuous of you, hiding behind your class and white-skin privilege, to urge others to violence."

With sparks flying from his eyes, he sputtered, "You have no idea what it will really take to overthrow the power structure. You and your wimpy husband will be left on the ash heap of history when the revolution comes."

"Spoken like a real garbage mouth," Mary pugnaciously flung at him.

Trying to deflect Mary's anger, Ted meekly offered one of his favorite quotes from Chairman Mao: "Well, you know power does grow out of the barrel of a gun."

Mary did not spare her host from her withering look, saying, "Ted, you don't even own a gun, and, if you did, how are you going to shoot it when you're high most of the time?"

That shut down Ted.

Before retreating Himmelfarb once more launched an attack on Mary, this time doubling down on his sexism. "The only power you'll ever have," sneering in her direction, "is pussy power."

Frank had to restrain her from attempting to do more than verbal damage to Himmelfarb. By midnight Mary was recovered from that angry exchange and much more relaxed after imbibing several glasses of wine. When the countdown to midnight found them together in a corner of the living room, they kissed until Marsha emerged from the kitchen with a large carrot cake in her hands. Encouraging everyone to join in singing "Happy Birthday" to Mary, Marsha placed the homemade cake on a large living room table and began cutting up slices to hand out to the assembled. She warned all about to consume the cake of a special ingredient she had put into the cream cheese frosting. For those who didn't immediately recognize what those little green flecks in that white frosting were, within the hour they and everyone else were as high as kites on a windy spring day.

One of the other guests at the New Year's Eve get-together was the legendary local radical, David Marvinoff. A former Freedom Rider and long-time pacifist, David ran a little shop selling goods produced in the South by those Blacks still connected to the unfinished work of the civil rights movement. David's new project, the Honeywell Action Project (H.A.P.), grew out of those discussions in Ted and Marsha's living room. Soon, he had pulled together a coalition of interested faculty, students, clergy, women's liberation, and draft resisters to lay the groundwork for a campaign against Honeywell's production of anti-personnel fragmentation bombs. Frank joined the campaign, taking on some research responsibilities and trying to organize a labor committee that would tap into any sympathetic workers at the large suburban plant where Honeywell produced many of those weapons in order to foment resistance to such production within the factory.

Meanwhile, Frank was also trying to secure a factory job, not for purposes of stirring up shop-floor militancy but to help pay the bills, especially with the looming possibility of being sent to prison and leaving Mary without any savings. At first, his applications were rejected without any serious consideration, let alone an interview. He realized that listing his educational background was literally a red flag to prospective employers who were on the lookout for student radicals coming into their shops and stirring up trouble. So, Frank started lying about his education. Almost immediately, he got an interview with the owner of a small rubber factory in South Minneapolis. In order to allay any suspicions about his motives for taking the job, he made up a story about his wife's pregnancy and myriad debts and bills that had to be paid. Frank got the job.

Working in a factory at hard labor starting at 7 A.M. was not a novel experience for this former Pittsburgher. He had worked in the Jones & Laughlin steel mill on the South Side of town during the two summers between his freshman and junior years at the University of Pittsburgh. One dismal difference between that past and the present job was the frigid Minnesota winters and the ever-present cold darkness that enveloped his drives to and from the rubber factory. Although Frank often worked in solitary assignments in the steel mill, there were many more occasions when he worked with other men in concert unlike the near complete isolation in this job. Another striking dissimilarity was the presence of women in the rubber factory. Among those women was an older chain-smoking sinewy character who could toss around one-hundred-pound bales of rubber as if they were one of the cartons of cigarettes she invariably carried in her pocket. Frank was in awe of her strength, but also hoped to gain her as an ally in his effort to unionize this non-union plant.

His organizing attempt in the small rubber factory proved as quixotic as the effort to form an alliance with dissident Teamsters in the suburban Honeywell plant that Frank and his H.A.P. comrades leafleted. That Teamsters local had raided the old United Electrical (U.E.) workers union at Honeywell during the Cold War when red baiting left-wing organizations was at its height. A few U.E. old-timers had actually contacted H.A.P. asking for more information and flyers to pass out inside the plant. The Teamsters union officials, however, made clear their antagonism to the whole project even after David explained in a tense meeting in early March 1969 that this wasn't about busting up the local or eliminating jobs. Quoting from one of the staple H.A.P. leaflets, he underscored the project's commitment to conversion to peacetime production without any loss of jobs. This reference didn't allay the suspicions and animosity of the Teamsters.

The hostility by the Teamsters local leadership was even more evident when the first meeting for union and community members in early summer attracted a union goon squad, consisting of tire-iron wielding and ominous-looking barrel-chested and beer-bellied figures who stood outside the gathering place intimidating all who wanted to enter. Very few people attended. When Frank endeavored to explain the purpose of the meeting to the sparse number of attendees, the few Teamsters in the audience began to boo and cause a ruckus. He was relieved when they abruptly stood up and exited, especially since he had no interest in becoming a target for a tire-iron.

Back in March David and two University of Minnesota professors had a more cordial and less threatening meeting with the Chairman of the Board of Honeywell in his well-appointed office at company headquarters in Minneapolis. Marvinoff laid out the non-negotiable demand that Honeywell immediately stop production of the fragmentation bombs and any other war material. Just to make his point about how heinous these weapons manufactured by his company were, David drew out from his briefcase a few grisly photographs of the Vietnamese victims of these bombs. The Chairman politely declined to view them, acknowledging his familiarity with the effects of the anti-personnel ordnance. When he took refuge in the fact that Honeywell had a contract with the Pentagon that couldn't be broken, Marvinoff politely pointed out that he and the company could expect demonstrations, and some civil disobedience, not only at the headquarters in Minneapolis, but at factories in Minnesota, around the country, and at Honeywell offices around the world.

As a follow-up to David's promise of demonstrations, the scattering of a few dozen protestors who made their first appearance at the end of April 1969 at Honeywell headquarters in Minneapolis would blossom into 1500 demonstrators marching from a nearby park in April 1970 to those offices where they blocked the entrances, preventing a meeting of the board and stockholders. The night before in a massive outdoor rally against Honeywell at Macalester College in St. Paul, Jerry Rubin in a militantly loopy address ranted to the 3500 in attendance, "We're gonna make Honeywell stop makin' bombs and go back to makin' honey." The next day at the confrontation at Honeywell headquarters, honey did not flow. Instead, the Minneapolis cops, eager to use their new pepper spray weapon, unleashed it on the unsuspecting protestors after a small group of irate young people had smashed the glass doors to the offices. Frank had his first, but not last, bitter taste of that awful gas.

If April ended with a despondent Frank tearing up from pepper spray, the beginning of the month commenced with real personal and political hope. On April 5 and 6, Easter weekend, mass demonstrations in New York, Chicago, and San Francisco brought out hundreds of thousands of antiwar protestors. In cities, large and small, including the Twin Cities, Quakers and other pacifist groups sat-in at draft boards. Then, in mid-April, Frank received a reprieve from sentencing when the U. S. Supreme Court accepted for review a case to which his was bound. Only a few days earlier, he and Mary had driven to Sandstone Penitentiary, the federal prison about one hundred miles north of Minneapolis, to which he would have most likely been sent for a minimum of two years. They drove right up to the gate, stopped and turned around without saying anything. When he heard from his lawyer about the Supreme Court's intention to consider the constitutionality of his and other's draft resistance, he was both relieved and excited to have more time with Mary, his political work, and even another more meaningful job.

The daily drudgery of working in the rubber factory had reminded him of how oppressive such mindless labor could be. He certainly felt little more than one of the slaves of developed industrial civilization that Marcuse had written about in *One-Dimensional Man.* Even his halting efforts to develop a modicum of solidarity with his fellow workers did not translate into what he hoped would be an organized effort to unionize the shop. His brief and limited discussions with Jenny, the older Amazonian woman who handled the heavy labor with amazing aplomb, never amounted to more than some common griping about the work.

There was little regret and much relief when he announced that he was quitting. He had given some thought to providing management a pretext to fire him, especially after he found out that some of the foam rubber casing he was helping to produce was intended for packaging Honeywell's fragmentation bombs. His furtive sabotage of that casing consisted of tearing a slice of the foam rubber in the hopes that this small imperfection would somehow lead to damaging the bomb and, thereby, preventing its use. However, he could never admit what he had done. Nor could he find another justification for being fired or laid off. So, he left with a week's notice and enough savings for a summer hiatus until he could find another job.

Dividing his time between the Honeywell Action Project and TCDAC work, Frank also took the opportunity to search for more challenging and rewarding employment. When he saw a posting at the University for a counselor/teacher in a new program in the General College, he immediately applied.

Within the week after submitting his application, he got a call to come in for an interview.

The two interviewers were the white male Assistant Dean of the General College and the Black female Director of the new program, Higher Education for Poor People, or H.E.P.P. As a consequence of the impact of the Poor People's campaign in the summer of 1968 and the occupation of Morrill Hall by university Black students in the late fall of that year, the University initiated a number of new programs, including H.E.P.P. As explained to Frank in the interview, the students being recruited for this General College two-year degree would be mostly older women, many of whom were single parents and eligible for Title IV funding to help underwrite their college expenses. After a short overview of the program, the Director asked the first and most obvious question.

"So, Mr. Goodman, why do you want this position and what makes you particularly suited for it?"

Although Frank had been expecting something along these lines, he still had to collect himself before answering.

"I realize I might not have the life experiences to relate to the majority of students being recruited for this program. On the other hand, both as an undergraduate and graduate student, I have demonstrated a commitment to fight for the underdog. My work with young Black kids at the Freedom School in Pittsburgh, where I also taught a more inclusive American history course, has given me some preparation for this job."

Quick to point out the obvious, the Director followed with "But these are adults. And mostly older Black women. How do you relate to them?"

"By treating them with dignity, making them co-creators of their educational experience and listening to what they have to say."

The Director nodded and turned to the Assistant Director. "Well, he certainly doesn't sound like his approach is missionary work or wanting to be a white savior."

A few days later Frank was notified that he got the position and would be starting in the fall with a one-year contract for the 1969-1970 academic year.

Thirty-Two

JULY 28, 1995

As Ruth Browne was waiting for Jane Rose, her psychiatrist co-worker and most likely new Director of S.A.V.E., she slowly sipped her white wine and reflected on her last day at the women's shelter in Jackson, Michigan. The battered mother and daughter who sought refuge as she was leaving for her dinner date with Jane were stark reminders that the mayhem of domestic violence was not going away. The horrible images and compelling life stories would remain with her even as she retreated to an academic life at the University of Toronto where she vowed to herself to translate those lives into her scholarly research as a doctoral candidate in Women's Studies and Sociology. Looking forward to starting graduate school in the fall of 1995 in the bucolic setting of Queens Park in Toronto, Ruth could not shake the feeling that she had not done enough during her three years as Director of S.A.V.E.

She spotted Jane entering the restaurant and waved to her. The slightly built Black woman who sauntered to the booth that Ruth occupied radiated an air of self-confidence and self-possession.

“I see you are drinking a glass of white wine. Is that your first? If so, let me buy you the next one. You might need it.”

“I know,” Ruth commented. “I’m wallowing in nostalgia and self-pity for my failures.”

“Didn’t count on this being a counseling session for you. I was hoping we could just celebrate all you had accomplished in your time as Director.”

“I don’t feel like I made a dent in the pandemic of domestic violence.”

Jane sighed. “Did you really think you were going to solve this international problem from this little outpost in Jackson?”

“Of course not. I just wanted to reverse the trends and that hasn’t seemed to happen.”

“Listen, Ruth, your work was invaluable, but you are not the white savior for all those victimized by sexual and domestic violence.”

“I never intended to come off as a ‘savior.’ I just wanted to be able to heal women from the trauma inflicted on them.”

Jane shook her head. “If anyone failed, I have to say that my counsel only touched the surface of that trauma. The deep social and cultural roots that imprison women and men in these sociopathic situations is often beyond our capacities as individuals, even with the best of intentions.”

“Thank you for that.”

“And speaking of imprisonment, I have some good news and bad news to deliver.”

“Okay, start with the bad news.” Ruth held her breath.

"I can't take on the job as Director. So, I think Vicky should take over from her Assistant Director position. She'll be great."

Ruth was dumbstruck. She had assured herself that leaving the director's position for Jane would put her mind at rest. While she had confidence that Vicky could manage, this news only complicated her departure.

"Now, I could use that second drink. And maybe a third given what might be your good news."

After calling over the waitress and ordering another white wine for Ruth and a bourbon for herself, Jane took a minute before announcing her "good news."

"I've been given a joint position at the Wayne State Medical School and Hutzel Hospital to work with women patients suffering from various traumas."

"That's wonderful news, Jane. Why didn't you let me know you had applied?"

"Well, why didn't you share information about your own application to grad school?"

Ruth pondered the fairness of the question.

"I guess we both had a secret that couldn't be revealed until it became a reality. So, you're off to Detroit and I'm going to Toronto, but there's no reason we can't stay in touch."

"I was about to say the same thing. And, let's drink to that."

Thirty-Three

JUNE 1969

After opening a bottle of cheap champagne for drinks with Ted and Marsha to celebrate the recent reprieve from the Supreme Court and to drink to his new job as counselor/teacher in H.E.P.P, Frank offered a toast to Mary for her forbearance during these tense times.

"Thank you for putting up with me and my frantic worrisome behavior."

Mary smiled and downed her glass of the bubbly. Motioning for a refill, she lifted her plastic goblet.

"Let's drink this next round for the winding down of the war."

"Mary," Frank admonished her, "Tricky Dick is not winding it down. He's just trying to cool out the opposition by claiming that the troop withdrawals show he's ending the war. For all we know, he's probably preparing to expand the bombing. And it's for sure that he's going to up the repression. Just consider the talk he gave the other day at some god-forsaken university. What the hell was its name?"

With a puzzled look on his face, Ted offered the name. "Wasn't it General Beetle Bailey or something like that somewhere in South Dakota?"

Frank laughed out loud, remembering that the correct name of this remote college was General Beadle State College, probably one of the few campuses at which Nixon could safely speak.

Had they actually heard or read what Nixon declared on that tiny campus, they might not be inclined to celebrate. As reported in the *Washington Post* on June 4, the day after the President spoke in South Dakota, he denounced "the student who invades an administration building, roughs up the dean, rifles the files and issues 'non-negotiable demands.' We have the power to strike back if need be, and to prevail. The Nation has survived other attempts at insurrection. We can survive this." Nixon may have been obliquely referring to the 1968 April occupations at Columbia University or the 1969 April takeover of a building by Black students at Cornell. In any case, his administration would go on the warpath against antiwar students, enlisting the repressive apparatus of the state and prompting hardhat construction workers in May 1970 to pummel protestors.

Although it did seem like students were in an insurrectionary mode and mood in the summer of 1969, the student movement, and specifically, SDS, was splintering into hard-line factions that were degenerating into fantasies of revolution. Even Frank's commitment to non-violence was wavering as the Black Panther Party was becoming the target of government repression and shootouts with local police around the country. Unlike Alan Himmelfarb, he would not glibly mouth the slogan about "picking up the gun," especially since he detested guns and weapons of any kind.

"Okay, kids," Ted exclaimed, "I've also got some great news to share. My recently deceased granddad apparently had stashed away some money that, for unknown reasons, he decided to leave to me. And what that means is that Marsha and I will be moving to a large house not far from here."

Frank was crestfallen. He had gotten used to the weekend parties downstairs with Ted's weed and Marsha's delicacies.

Seeing the look on Frank's face, Marsha offered some solace by inviting Frank and Mary to a July 4th party at the new place. She even promised to bake another one of her carrot cakes for his birthday.

"Will it have the special ingredient in the cream cheese frosting?" asked Frank.

"You betcha," Mary replied.

"Another reason for buying a bigger domicile," Ted continued, "is my second wife is leaving the state and finally will be relinquishing her custody of my two daughters, Carly and Karen. So, they'll be joining us."

Marsha expressed her excitement about becoming a step mom and then warned Ted that all future parties would have to curtail the pot smoking, at least in the house.

"I'll miss having you downstairs," acknowledged Mary. "It was so easy to always borrow food from you, Marsha, whenever I ran out of something."

"Well, you can just do a hop, skip, and jump the few blocks down the street and still get what you need if you're ever in short supply. In the meantime, Mary, could you help me with the packing?"

"Absolutely."

The two couples parted. Frank broke the silence by musing over the question of whether they should also consider moving into a larger place, one that might have a real backyard with the possibility of a garden. Mary wasn't ready to undertake another relocation. However, she did propose to undertake a journey in the summer to visit relatives in Lake of the Woods, Minnesota.

"My two great aunts and uncle live on a farm near Warroad. We could drive up there and stay a few days. It's really pretty and might be a good time to take a little break."

Frank readily agreed, but was puzzled about the name of the place that Mary described as being so picturesque. It was only later that he learned about the origin of its designation as the "War-Trail" for the Ojibwa/Anishinaabe who once inhabited this region. Now, the remnants of the war-trail were transferred to the local arena where ice hockey became for kids and their parents a substitute for the aggression that in the past marred the dealings between the Sioux and Ojibwa.

The six-hour trip to Warroad was beautiful with pine trees lining part of the road. When they stopped at a forested rest area, they saw a moose, an animal he had never seen before in the wild. He was bowled over by the size of the creature. The moose's legs were much longer than he imagined and the antlers looked like deadly spears. Frank kept his distance. Unfortunately, he couldn't avoid being attacked by the pesky mosquitoes buzzing around the nearby small pond. They were as big as tiny birds and sounded like distant B-52 bombers. It reminded Frank that even this remote area was still part of the war-road that demarcated each and every region of the country.

When they arrived at the farm, the two elderly aunts, Margaret and Jenny, were waiting outside. Uncle Eric was in the barn. As Mary had explained, Jenny and her young son, Sean, had moved in with Margaret and Eric after her husband Danny, a railroad worker, was killed in a train accident during the Depression. Mary's Aunt Jenny, whose maiden name was O'Connell, had married Danny O'Donnell. The two O'Donnell grandsons were both in the military; Jon, the older, was in the Marines and had fought in Vietnam and was now stationed in Thailand, and Marc, the younger, was in the Navy.

Frank slowed the Corvair down and, then, parked close to the barn. Exiting the car, Mary ran towards both aunts, giving hugs to each. Both had care-worn appearances with almost the exact same creases on their face. The two sisters cackled non-stop questions at Mary. Hearing the commotion, Eric came out of the barn, strode towards Mary and embraced her. If Eric had added one hundred pounds to his weight and grown his grizzled white beard much longer, he would definitely have resembled a good version of St. Nick. As they all stood looking at the longhaired lanky young man emerging from the dusty Corvair, Frank drew the suitcases out of the trunk. Eric came forward to help.

"So, you're the young man who married our Mary. Can you handle her spunk?"

"I'm trying, but not always succeeding."

The two aunts hurried Mary into the house, pointing in the direction of the guest bedroom where she and her husband would sleep for the next two nights. Delicious smells, emanating from the kitchen, greeted Frank as he crossed the doorway to the old homestead.

Giving Frank the other suitcase, the red-necked Eric suggested taking the suitcases to the bedroom and freshening up before dinner. Once inside the bedroom, he joined Mary on the creaky bed.

"I guess we'll have to forget about having sex with the noise that this bed makes."

"There's always a nice haystack in the barnyard."

"Yeh, and all of those sensual smells of manure to induce love-making."

She smiled. "If it works for the horses, I'm sure you could get it up even in those circumstances."

He laughed. They kissed. Then, both found the bathroom to wash their hands and throw some water on their faces.

At dinner and for the next two days, Frank and Mary were regaled by family stories, especially the tales that Eric told about his misadventures in World War I, having first been taken for a German spy before being sent off at the very end of the war to the bloody trenches in France. Returning with all his limbs intact, he got a job in a slaughterhouse in St. Paul where he later lost two fingers on his left hand before taking up farming and marrying Margaret. That loss certainly didn't impede his ability, even at his advanced age of seventy, to toss around bales of hay or to milk the one cow that lived in the barn.

When Frank and Mary snuck into the barn later that first evening on the farm, Bessie, as the cow was called, resorted to loud mooing, interrupting Frank and Mary's aborted attempt at lovemaking on one of the stacks of hay. The next morning both found small slivers of straw matted in their hair.

"Wonder why Bessie was so riled last night?" Eric queried with a twinkle in his eyes.

Frank turned the color of Eric's neck and coughed in embarrassment. It was Jenny who immediately followed up by asking Mary when she planned to have a child.

"Well, we're still young and we've got time."

Not particularly pleased with that excuse, Jenny came right back at Mary. "You don't want to wait too long. You never know what can happen."

Mary glanced at Frank who was diligently applying himself to the consumption of his bacon and eggs, pretending not to have heard the conversation. He continued to remain oblivious to the matter when Mary raised it on their way back home. When they pulled up to their duplex in South Minneapolis, they noticed a "For Rent" sign in the window of the empty downstairs apartment. Without speaking, they took their belongings and the cookies the aunts had baked for them into their upstairs apartment where they were greeted by silence.

Thirty-Four

MID-SEPTEMBER 1969

The noise was deafening. It didn't help that the acoustics in this tiny old high-ceiling classroom were non-existent. Even with up-to-date sound absorption materials, the authoritative voices of the women in the room would have dominated the space. That there were only sixteen students in the class, fourteen of them women, could not deter the loud conversation that bounced off the walls, piercing the eardrums of the mesmerized instructor. To say this particular aggregation of students intimidated him would have been an understatement. He tentatively asked them to re-arrange their chairs so they formed a circle. This helped quiet them and settle him down.

Frank had already come into contact with a number of the dozen Black women who sat before him. Among the most talkative in the classroom was Ronnie Hammer, one of those he met earlier in the week for a counseling session. During that meeting, she had told him of participating in the Poor People's Campaign in July 1968. Ms. Hammer recounted the words of the President of the National Welfare Rights Organization (NWRO), of which she was the leader in the Twin Cities, in order to re-emphasize its diversity and its focus. Quoting from Johnnie Tillmon's speech from last summer in D.C., this single mom with a stentorian voice repeated the following: "We are black and white, Mexican, Puerto Rican, and Indian. We are together and we have our own special kind of power. That power is Mother Power. We will fight for the welfare of our children." There was no way to doubt the sincerity of that pledge, whether articulated by Johnnie Tillmon or re-articulated by Ronnie Hammer.

Ms. Hammer was one of the older and definitely heavier Black women in the class. She looked strong enough to have punched out any of the mounted cops and their horses that had trampled protesting NWRO women this past summer in New York City. According to her application, which Frank had reviewed, she was forty-five, born in the Depression in Alabama and brought by her parents to Minneapolis during World War II. Having married and divorced, she had custody of two teenage sons, both now in high school. She had worked in an industrial laundromat before injuring herself in an accident on the job for which she now received workman's comp. Along with AFDC and Title IV money, she was able to handle her bills and enroll in H.E.P.P. courses.

In order to learn the names of the other students in the class, Frank encouraged each person to give an introduction that included the reason for wanting to sign up for this program in the General College. Almost all cited the need for a degree in order to get a good job or even a career. The two men, a Chicano named Roy Rojas, originally from Texas, and a very dark-skinned guy, native to Minnesota, who insisted on being called "X," were both Vietnam Vets. Neither said much in the way of an introduction other than being glad they were alive. Of the two white women in the class, the younger, a ravishing redhead in tight jeans at whom Frank tried not to stare, was Rachel Jones, a twenty-three-year-old mother of a five-year-old daughter.

As Frank would later learn through a number of counseling sessions, Rachel's boyfriend had gotten her pregnant during her senior year in high school, derailing her plans to get a university education. When her daughter was two, the boyfriend left for Alaska, foregoing further contact with Rachel. Now that the little girl was old enough to go to kindergarten, Rachel was hoping to convert her part-time waitress job to full-time.

After all of the introductions, Frank briefly laid out the course syllabus. He highlighted the use of the primary source material in the anthology that would constitute the bulk of the readings for the course. Next, he explained why the only other text, James Baldwin's non-fiction masterpiece, *The Fire Next Time*, was critical to demystifying the dominant historical narrative. Of course, his explanation for the use of the Baldwin book relied on more accessible language, emphasizing, in particular, the reference to the collective myths of that white-inflected history. Then, he paused to ask the first of a number of questions that would occupy the rest of the hour session.

"Why study history?"

Ronnie was, of course, first to respond. "To learn from the mistakes of the past."

"Just the mistakes? What about what people accomplished by making their own history in the past?"

Roy was quick to point out that history books don't often talk about the accomplishments of common people. "It's just the winners that write history. And the losers get written out, particularly when your land and history get stolen from you."

One of the other Black women agreed, saying, "I never read nothin' about my people other than they was slaves."

"You never heard about Sojourner Truth or Harriet Tubman?" Frank inquired.

Everyone, including Ronnie and Rachel, shook their heads.

"Well, we're going to read what they both said and did from the anthology of primary sources for this course."

Rachel ventured that reading the words of people who were not part of the traditional texts they had read in high school would be of value for its own sake. This insight allowed Frank to talk about the difference between the intrinsic and extrinsic value of education, reflecting back on the reasons that the students had cited for enrolling in the program.

He then handed out an excerpt from the Declaration of Independence, starting with the well-known passage: "We hold these truths to be self-evident, that all men are created equal, that they are endowed by their Creator with certain unalienable Rights, that among these are Life, Liberty, and the pursuit of Happiness." He divided the class into groups of four and had them read over and discuss what this passage and the later one about "the Right of the People to alter or abolish it" meant to them. Everyone seemed animated and fully engaged in the discussion.

After about fifteen minutes, Frank had them re-form the circle. He then asked what they knew about the author of the Declaration. Both Rachel and Ronnie said in unison, "He owned slaves." Just the point he wanted to have them cite in order to then inquire about why Jefferson, the slave-owner, could pen the words - "All men are created equal."

Roy couldn't resist: "He was a fuckin' hypocrite. Excuse my French, ladies."

Frank then interjected that even though Jefferson considered enslaved people of African descent to be less equal than whites, he also kept a light-skinned former house slave, Sally Hemings, as his concubine, fathering at least several children with her. Not one of the students had ever heard this although it prompted Roy once again to utter, "fuckin' hypocrite." To which Frank responded that maybe it was more complicated than hypocrisy. Maybe the whole edifice of white supremacy was based on a system of racial capitalism that trafficked in the bodies of enslaved people for profits. At this point, the Black Vietnam Vet muttered a subdued, "Right on!"

The utterance gave Frank an opportunity to ask "X" what he thought was meant by this excerpted passage from the Declaration of Independence – "That whenever any Form of Government becomes destructive of these ends, it is the Right of the People to alter or abolish it." "X" looked at his large calloused hands and then staring straight ahead, he muttered, "You got the right to rebel when the Man don't listen. And that's what the Second Amendment to the Constitution gives you. Your right, as some of the brothers say, to pick up the gun." Frank and the rest of the class were stunned into silence. On one hand, he wanted to acknowledge the insights of this Black Vietnam Vet. On the other hand, he was tempted to go into a more critical analysis of the Second Amendment, pointing out that the real motivation for it was to make sure that the individual states and their militias could be used for putting down any slave revolts and continuing the genocidal policies against native peoples. Instead, Frank solicited responses from the other students, adding that it was also Jefferson who wrote "that a little rebellion now and then is a good thing." To which "X" pointedly commented, "As long as it wasn't a rebellion of his slaves!" The class and Frank all guffawed.

Before he and the rest of the class knew it, the hour for class had expired. The students and Frank were pleasantly surprised about how quick the time went and how engaged they all had been. As they slowly filed out the door, many still in animated conversation, Rachel stayed behind.

"Any chance I can see you for a counseling session?"

"Sure," Frank replied, trying not to appear too eager to have the chance for a one-on-one exchange with her. "What time works best for you?"

"If you're available in the morning. I can drop my daughter off at kindergarten and get here before I have to go to work."

They agreed upon a 9:00 A.M. meeting on an upcoming Friday morning. Rachel said goodnight and started walking out the door. Frank tried not to stare after her, but couldn't avoid gazing at her seductive sexy gait.

Thirty-Five

EARLY SEPTEMBER 1995

"Freedom of movement." As she walked together with hundreds of other women on a balmy early September evening in the 1995 Toronto Take Back the Night march, Ruth recalled the phrase used by Andrea Dworkin in a TBTN demonstration in Los Angeles over fifteen years before. The fight for that freedom of movement still continued because rape culture and sexual violence persisted. The nighttime for women remained, as Dworkin so powerfully and poignantly declaimed then, like "playing Russian roulette." Along with the rest of the militant marchers, Ruth was committed to removing that gun from the heads of women here and everywhere.

She had only arrived in Toronto a few weeks before. Her graduate classes had just started. Ruth had hardly settled into the graduate housing in Queens Park when the flyers posted around campus alerted her to the Take Back the Night demonstration. Now, as she marched with women who were strangers to her on unfamiliar streets, she nonetheless felt the spirit that underlay the feminist slogan, "Sisterhood is Powerful." With her lighted candle joining with hundreds of others, the literal and figurative darkness was dispelled.

When the march made its way into a large open area, it stopped. A speaker's stage had been erected. Because Ruth was in the back, it was difficult to hear what was being said until Eileen Penny stepped up to the mic. In a booming voice, she denounced the male supremacist system that perpetuated sexual and domestic violence. Citing the damning statistics underlying the prevalence of rape, this soon-to-be Ph.D. from Minnesota lit up the crowd with even more intensity than that generated by the collection of candles. Ruth vowed to catch up to Eileen at the conclusion of the rally.

Wending her way through the crowd, she reached the front of the stage just as the final speaker had concluded. She spotted Eileen descending the stairs and approached her.

Holding out her hand, Ruth introduced herself to Eileen, "Hi, my name is Ruth Browne. I was born in Minneapolis, but left when I was three with my mom, Mary Browne. I…"

"Holy cow. Your mom was Mary Browne? I knew her in Minneapolis. An incredibly smart and savvy woman, definitely a feminist, if not as radical as I would have liked. How is she?"

"She passed away earlier this year from breast cancer."

"I'm so sorry to hear about that. It's so upsetting to know that there's really no sense of urgency in figuring out how to prevent breast cancer. Anyhow, I heard she wound up at Wayne State University after getting a Fulbright to Venice, Italy."

"Yeh, I basically grew up in Michigan, did my undergrad at the University of Michigan, and then worked the last three years as director of a women's shelter in Jackson, Michigan. Now I'm here on a fellowship in Women's Studies and Sociology to study domestic violence."

"Just what I'm writing my dissertation on. We've got to get together soon and have a much longer talk. I have to get back to my apartment."

"One final question before you go. My mom never really told me anything about my birth father other than he was a fellow grad student and they had a short romance before he left her. He didn't even know she was pregnant with me. And, apparently, they never communicated after he split. I found a marriage license in her papers that listed his name – Franklin Roosevelt Goodman."

"Holy shit! Frank Goodman is your birth father?"

"You knew him?"

"Knew him. He and I once got into a real angry exchange about strategy and tactics for the draft resistance movement. Even worse, he betrayed my brother, Jim, leaving him in the lurch to face criminal charges that ended in his incarceration. My brother came out of prison a basket case. That may have not been Frank's fault, but he certainly does have to answer for bugging out on my brother and the others in the "Minnesota Three." Looks like we'll need some extended time to discuss all of this. How about next weekend coming over to my apartment for the day?"

"I'd love to. Give me your telephone number and I'll give you a ring."

"I'll be waiting for your call."

Ruth took the TBTN flyer out of the back pocket of her jeans and handed it to Eileen. Scribbling her contact info on the sheet of paper, the short, rotund, and round-faced feminist firebrand delivered more than just a telephone number and a stirring speech to Ruth. She held out a key to some of the missing parts of Ruth's identity.

Thirty-Six

LATE SEPTEMBER 1969

Eileen Penny couldn't believe what she heard Frank Goodman just advocate.

"You want to break into Selective Service offices now as we're building an even bigger draft resistance movement this fall? With the demonstrations coming up in October and November?"

Looking around the TCDAC office for support from his fellow draft resisters against this female interloper, he appealed to Dan, John, Fred, and even Jim, hoping that the sibling connection wouldn't overrule their fellowship.

"We can do both," he vehemently argued. "While we're mobilizing new people and recruiting more guys into turning in their draft cards, we can up our own commitment to more radical civil disobedience, like the Catonsville Nine and Milwaukee Fourteen."

"Jesus Christ," she responded. "You really do have a martyr complex!"

"God," Frank angrily replied. "I hear enough of that accusation from Mary. I don't need to have that baseless charge flung at me here at the TCDAC and especially by someone not facing prison as a consequence of defying the Selective Service System."

Eileen roared back at him, "Yeh, well, if the draft wasn't so sexist, I'd also be a resister. Instead, you guys circulate this crap about 'Girls say Yes to Boys who say No!'" It makes me want to puke."

Neither Frank nor any of the other men gathered there felt inclined to comment. Although it would be hard to call any of these fellows feminists, they were all embarrassed by that slogan. The silence was broken when Eileen got up from her chair and left the office in a huff.

As he watched his sister depart, Jim spoke haltingly but directly facing Frank. "I think you might want to consider apologizing to Eileen. She puts in a ton of time for the TCDAC and I think you probably hurt her feelings."

"Maybe I will," Frank lied. "Anyhow, I have to admit that it probably makes sense to wait to do an action until after the upcoming mobilizations and draft card turn-in."

"You might also want to find out what the Supreme Court is going to do with our cases," Dan remarked. "I mean, you, Jim, and I, are all tied together with that draft case before the Court. Let's postpone any discussion of another attack on the Selective Service System until we hear what our fate might be."

Frank grudgingly acknowledged the logic of Dan's comments.

"Just one final point about the future deliberation of a raid on any local draft board. I don't think we should stick around to be arrested. I don't want to go to jail in Nixon's America."

"Then, you're not talking about civil disobedience since the underlying principle is accepting the punishment by the state for breaking a law, even an unjust one."

"I understand, Dan. But what I'm proposing is more like political sabotage – a sort of hit-and-run in order to escape the law."

At this point, Jim piped up. "Look, can we just table this for now. I'm willing to discuss this after we have a better sense of what's happening to us and to the anti-draft and antiwar movement."

All nodded in agreement.

Fred had wanted to say something, but had held back until the atmosphere cleared. Standing up from his chair for added emphasis, he pulled a shiny object out of his pocket. It looked like a key, but with a round band attached to it.

"I need to go back to Moorhead, but this time by myself. During the six months that Stan and I remained in that region, a faculty member from Concordia College with whom we worked insisted that I come back in the fall. He gave me this key ring as an inducement to return. I promised I would come up by October. So, I'll be leaving in a few days."

"How long do you plan on staying?" Dan inquired.

"Don't know for sure, but I may not be back for a while."

All were quiet, trying to fathom what it would mean for their fellowship if Fred were permanently gone. No one ventured to dissuade him from his journey north even as they were already feeling the loss.

Thirty-Seven

FALL 1969

It didn't take much effort on Frank's part to convince Mary of the move to North Minneapolis. Almost every day during September, the father of the family in the apartment downstairs would beat either his wife or his seven-year old son. On several occasions when the screaming was particularly upsetting, Frank had attempted to confront the father only to be told to mind his own business. Finally, after a blood-curdling row between husband and wife, Mary called the police. The cops did nothing more than issue a warning to the father. That was when they decided to find another place to live.

Relocating to North Minneapolis in an area that was predominantly occupied by working class Black families was a combination of choice and chance. When Frank mentioned to the Director of H.E.P.P. that he and his wife were thinking about moving to North Minneapolis, she told him about a house for rent down the block from where her sister lived. Mary was much more tentative about the area until she saw the sturdy two-story wooden structure with a large back yard that could easily accommodate an extensive vegetable garden. Added to this inducement was the fact that Mary had almost completed her course work for the doctorate and would be spending less time on campus, especially since the fall term would be her last for a teaching assistantship in the English Department. As it turned out, she obtained a part-time teaching position at a trade college in North Minneapolis, within walking distance of their prospective new abode.

Frank was eager for the move because Ronnie Hammer had told him of the possibility of using the basement of the Baptist church that housed the offices of the Minneapolis chapter of the National Welfare Rights Organization as a site for a tutoring program on the weekends for interested women from the NWRO. Because she was enthusiastic about the idea and accepted the fact that this tall longhaired white guy might have something to offer, she began to drum up support for a tutoring program. For his part, Frank was self-conscious about being some kind of white missionary. So, he promised himself that whatever he would teach would grow organically out of the needs of those who showed up. As it turned out, everyone among them needed some tutoring in reading and writing skills, which he was happy to do in one-on-one sessions. At first, there were only about a half-dozen women, all Black with the exception of a dark-skinned Puerto Rican single mom, Isabella, who brought along her ten-year-old son, Jose. He immediately connected with the kid since they both shared a love of baseball and worshipped Roberto Clemente, the all-star right fielder for the Pittsburgh Pirates who just happened to be Puerto Rican.

Isa proved to be a quick and competent learner, probably because her reading and writing capabilities were already fairly well developed. Frank also had to admit to himself that the pleasure of tutoring her extended beyond the student-teacher boundary. Both were aware that there was a physical attraction. Neither, however, wanted to act on transgressing the border that separated the pedagogical experience from a different, and more intimate, intercourse.

The same couldn't be said about Frank's growing involvement with Rachel. The weekly counseling conferences went quickly from academic to very personal matters. He knew that these exchanges were becoming more intense and illicit as they explored a wide range of topics, including issues of sexuality. As much as Frank tried to hold back, he found himself willingly and openly sharing the frustrations about his sex life or lack thereof with Mary. Rachel, in turn, expressed her own disappointments with men who never really took into account her intelligence or her passion about the world beyond bodily gratifications. He nightly dreamed and daily desired such physical indulgences with her, but was reluctant to act on those desires until the winter when the stigma of being his student was removed. Then, the indiscretion of the affair became caught up in the lies he told to Mary and the ultimate betrayal of their marriage bonds.

Those bonds were fraying in the fall of 1969. Mary was distracted with her finishing her Ph.D. course work and her part-time teaching at the trade school. Frank's involvement with H.E.P.P. as a counselor and teacher and the ongoing political work at the TCDAC and the Honeywell Action Project undercut his commitment to nurturing the relationship. The estrangement both experienced made for an unhappy existence as a couple.

Thirty-Eight

FALL 1995

The delight that both Ruth and Eileen took in being a couple was evident to all who witnessed their appearances at political and social events. By all measurements, especially the physical ones, they were a rather odd couple. Eileen, over twenty years older than Ruth, was short and chubby with close-cropped hair of alternate streaks of pink and purple. Her much taller partner was rather thin with long blonde-brunette hair. Together, they embodied an uncomedic feminist version of Abbott and Costello, always knowing who was on first, second, and third. They started finishing each other's sentences, especially when the subject was sexual and domestic violence. One would cite a statistic about the under-reporting by women of rape while the other would note the domestic abuse of the spouses of police officers was more than forty percent higher than other wives. The fall term at the University of Toronto, the first for Ruth but the penultimate for Eileen, was immensely gratifying for both, not only because of their intimacy but also because of their intellectual pursuits.

One of their favorite pastimes, when there wasn't a march or rally to organize or attend, was to spend a whole Saturday afternoon at one of the myriad bookstores that bordered the campus. On this particular crisp fall day they decided to venture further away from campus, seeking out previously unexplored areas of town. Heading up Bathurst Street towards the Jewish neighborhood, they first encountered a used bookstore that had a variety of volumes stacked in the front window. Eileen beckoned Ruth to follow her inside. Finding a section labeled "Feminist Studies," they perused the shelves.

Eileen let out a little squeal as she pulled out one of the titles near the bottom.

"Wow, this looks like a virgin copy of *The Dialectic of Sex*. You've read it, of course," she queried Ruth.

Sheepishly Ruth responded, "Not really. I mean I think I heard about Shulamith Firestone, but never read this book."

Eileen just shook her head. "You youngsters don't have any regard for the feminist pioneers and their classic works. It's all about intersectionality now. You need to go back to explore some of these foundational texts of radical feminism."

Ruth didn't want to argue about whose version of radical feminism was more inclusive. Instead, she invited Eileen to instruct her in some of the basics of the Firestone book.

Eileen was happy to oblige, pointing out how Firestone's *The Dialectic of Sex* built on Simone de Beauvoir's *The Second Sex* and the critique of "uterine oppression."

Sounding academically didactic, Eileen continued with her mini-lecture. "According to Firestone, in order to seize control of reproduction, women had to do more than eliminate male supremacy. They had to end the sex distinction itself."

"Whoa. Hold on. How is that possible?"

"By technological means."

"You mean there would be no more natural childbirth. It would be all artificial?"

"If you want to end uterine oppression, you've got to rely on technological intervention. Haven't you read Marge Piercy's utopian novel, *Woman on the Edge of Time?*

"No, I haven't, but I have a feeling you're going to make me read that also."

"Piercy's vision of the future society in Mattapoisett is where children are birthed by machines and men, get this, grow breasts to help breast feed and raise these artificial kids."

"Not sure I'm down with all that, but it does sound really intriguing."

"Okay. I'm buying you the Firestone and seeing if I can locate a copy of the Piercy novel."

Having purchased *The Dialectic of Sex*, but not finding a used copy of *Woman on the Edge of Time*, Eileen suggested that they continue their stroll up Bathurst. After traversing a few blocks and checking out the different shops on their way, Ruth, who was a few steps ahead of Eileen, noticed a large banner outside a store on the other side of the street. Above the banner with the words, "Grand Opening," emblazoned on it was a black and red sign that spelled out "The Rebel." Ruth motioned to Eileen to follow her. Even before they reached the front, it was obvious that they had discovered another bookstore.

Eileen eagerly entered through the front door, looking for the fiction section. "I'm going to see if they have the Piercy book," she said as she wandered into the rows of literature.

Ruth stopped at the front desk where she found a stack of flyers announcing monthly Friday author's talks. Many of the names were somewhat unfamiliar to her, perhaps because they were Canadian writers. However, the last name on the list and the one that jumped out at her was Camille Paglia. Paglia's new book, *Vamps and Tramps*, was already drawing the ire of radical feminists that Ruth respected. What she knew of Paglia's work on rape culture often sounded to her like a rationalization for its existence and persistence.

As a young woman clerk approached, Ruth was trying to tamp down the growing anger she was experiencing over the Paglia listing for an Author's Talk on June 28, 1996.

Ruth spat out her inquiry, "Are you the owner?"

"No, he's not here now. He might be at his wife's restaurant a mile up the street."

"What's his name?" Ruth asked with barely suppressed fury.

Sensing the rage that this customer was projecting, the clerk hesitated to give up the owner's name. "Why do you want to know?"

"If you can't tell me his name, at least let him know that having Camille Paglia speak at this bookstore is an invitation to picketing by me and my feminist sisters."

"I guess that's your right to demonstrate, but I don't understand why you'd do this since what I know of Paglia's writings is that she considers herself a feminist."

"Yeh, an anti-feminist," Ruth spat out with disgust. "I don't plan to patronize this store if that's the kind of speaker that "The Rebel" thinks the public wants to hear."

"Well, that's your opinion and we're all entitled to our opinion."

"Except for rapists and other violent victimizers of women's bodies."

With that final verbal salvo, Ruth turned and exited the bookstore, forgetting even that Eileen was still inside. When she emerged, she held up a new copy of *Women on the Edge of Time*. Ruth was tempted to tell her to return it immediately. Seeing the smile on Eileen's face as she handed Ruth the Piercy novel mollified her anger.

Thirty-Nine

FALL 1969

The anger that spilled into the streets of downtown Chicago in early October 1969 under the rubric of "Days of Rage" was an expression of the revolutionary wrath that fueled the small SDS sect known as "Weatherman". The militant madness of this action was marginal to the massive mobilizations that would take place later in October and November. Frank and his comrades at the TCDAC were especially focused on building towards another march to the Old Federal Building in downtown Minneapolis in mid-November where, they hoped, there would be a large rally and draft card turn-in. For the most part, Frank remained in the background while John Rider took on the role as the public face of draft resistance in Minnesota.

Now in his senior year at the "U," Rider had shed much of his physical identity as well as divesting himself of his draft card. Transformed from the all-American crew-cut kid who Frank first saw in September 1967 into a longhaired hippie, Rider, nonetheless, still insisted on wearing tight-hugging tshirts, even in the chilly fall season. The incongruity of the hirsute appearance with his muscle clothing may have bothered an older generation. To young men and women of Rider's age, his charismatic identity, mixing up oppositional markers of masculinity, wowed youthful audiences. It also helped that he was a very effective speaker at high school and college forums.

Throughout the month of September and into early October, John Rider visited a number of high school and college campuses in the greater Twin Cities. At every venue, whether a large assembly or a small meeting, he touted the upcoming Moratorium in October and November and encouraged local leadership to plan some sort of action. Little did he, or his comrades at the TCDAC, imagine that these two events would mobilize several million across the country. Among those activated were students at more than a thousand high schools. The rally that emerged in Minneapolis drew fifteen thousand, many of them new to antiwar protest. The following month's anti-draft demonstration brought more than 3000 to the Old Federal Building where John welcomed more than a dozen into the fellowship of draft resisters. For the first time there was participation by active duty military, including an Army PFC who, in removing his hat and coat, pledged to refuse cooperation with what he called the "war club."

Around this same time in November, a story surfaced of a horrible atrocity committed by members of the U.S. war club in Vietnam. Although this slaughter of nearly five hundred unarmed men, women, and children happened in March of 1968, it took over a year and half before the mainstream media discovered the "My Lai Massacre." While Frank knew that the atrocities perpetrated against innocent Vietnamese by extensive U.S. bombing made those on the ground almost pale into insignificance, the pictures from My Lai of women, children, and even babies strewn over the bloody ground and the lack of accountability for those in command sickened him.

Raging against Nixon and the whole war machine even in the privacy of his home only made Mary more uncomfortable in his company.

"Did you see those photographs of the littered dead bodies murdered in our name? How can you stand living in this country now, Mary?"

"Those pictures are everywhere and it's stirring the conscience of the American people."

"Hah," he bitterly responded. "I saw a poll that was taken by *Time* magazine of Americans who had seen the images from My Lai. You know what percentage of those in the survey claimed not to be upset by the massacre? Go ahead, take a guess."

Mary hated it when Frank asked her this kind of question, knowing that she would always answer with a percentage that was way off the mark. So, this time she inflated her response. "Fifty percent."

"Close, but no cigar. It was sixty-five percent. Sixty-five percent of the American people were not bothered by this slaughter even after seeing the photographs."

Mary thought about challenging his reference to the "American people," especially since it was a poll of a select sample. She realized, however, that his tirade would not admit of any nuance. She said nothing more.

He took her silence as assent. "See, even you know this country is without redemption. I should 'light out for the territory.' Namely, head north to Canada."

For this remark, she couldn't resist making an obvious comment. "You're not Huck Finn, even though you act like an adolescent orphan."

Frank just glared at her for a moment and then left the room.

When he met his H.E.P.P. history class the following week, he retained his bitterness. The assignment for that session seemed to be perfectly in sync with his mood. James Baldwin's *The Fire Next Time* was an excoriating jeremiad, laying bare the white blind spot in the mythic narrative of "heroic" American history. Eliciting the reaction of his students to the text, Frank focused in particular on the following passage:

The American Negro has the great advantage of having never believed the collection of myths to which white Americans cling: that their ancestors were all freedom-loving heroes, that they were born in the greatest country the world has ever seen, or that Americans are invincible in battle and wise in peace, that Americans have always dealt honorably with Mexicans (here Roy interrupted with a loud and ironic, "Yeh, right!) and Indians and all other neighbors or inferiors, that American men are the world's most direct and virile (here most of Black women just uttered – "Um hem"), that American women are pure (to which Ronnie added – "Yeh, pure as white snow," emphasizing "white.")

Baldwin's words and the whole text just opened the floodgates of grievances, rushing like the nearby Mississippi River after a torrential rain. Frank tried to steer the conversation back into some interpretive eddies, but was overwhelmed by the raging rivulets of righteous resentments.

Even after the time had elapsed for the regular class, students were still engaged in deep discussion. Frank had to remind them that they needed to vacate the room, hoping that Rachel would not follow his instructions. She didn't. She stayed. They engaged in some meaningless banter for a while about the term. Then, they stopped talking. The longing that pulsed through them had reached a breaking point. The boundaries were collapsing.

Forty

WINTER 1970

Crossing the border dividing North Minneapolis from the contiguous suburb of Columbia Heights, Frank realized that this geographical boundary, lined with icy streets on a cold January morning, would be the least problematical to navigate. The pre-arranged tryst at Rachel's apartment triggered what would become an avalanche of lies over the next few snowy winter months and into the spring. Each Saturday that he drove to spend a blissful time with Rachel added another layer of guilt on top of the falsehoods with which he blanketed Mary. The deceit created an even more dreadful estrangement in his married life. All the while, the libidinal lure of being with someone whose intense sexuality was like a seductive drug overcame the mortification he felt when lying in bed at night next to Mary.

Sex with Mary, never very fulfilling and often confounded by his immaturity and inadequacies, withered to nothing. With Rachel, his body came alive as she led him through all of the ways to make her climax. He was ecstatic that they mutually explored a variety of positions, none of which, fortunately, relapsed into the missionary one. The bubble that he inhabited with her, continually fogged by their passionate discharges, was finally punctured in the early spring when she announced that she would be leaving to rejoin her husband in San Diego where he now worked at a well-paying job in a defense plant. Frank was shocked not only because he was led to believe that they weren't legally married, but also for the loss of this satiating pleasure.

Almost pleading with her in an unmanly whiny voice, he cried, "Do you have to go?"

"I need to re-connect with the father of my daughter. I owe it to him and myself to see if we can make a go of it this time."

He tried to hide his despondency. He knew he was being selfish. He also couldn't imagine finding another sexual being as sensuous as Rachel. Staring into her brown eyes, so vividly set off by her red hair, he knew not to beg her to stay. For what was he prepared to offer her beyond an illicit affair with a married man? And so, they separated.

For Frank, the end of the relationship with Rachel occurred at the nadir of his life with Mary. The wedge that he drove into his marriage by the affair and his morose moods about the political situation led to an inevitable dissolution of the marriage. Even the Supreme Court decision, rendered during the winter of 1970, finding that Frank and the other draft resisters who had returned their Selective Service cards were protected by the First Amendment's "freedom of speech" clause could not repair the breach between him and Mary. And so, they drifted further apart as the snowdrifts piled even higher into late March.

Forty-One

APRIL TO JUNE 1970

By April 1970, the antiwar movement seemed locked into an imposed hibernation. Nixon's tricky "Vietnamization" policy, with large U.S. troop withdrawals, gained popular support even as the draft lottery adopted at the end of 1969 took a lot of the air out of the resistance. There were, however, attacks on Selective Service offices around the country, including in Twin Cities where the so-called "Muskrat 44" raided two offices, destroying thousands of files in the process. Other militants who considered themselves the "vanguard of the revolution" unleashed a rash of bombings in February and March. In early March a townhouse in Greenwich Village, housing a group of Weatherman, was destroyed, killing three when the bomb that was being constructed in the basement exploded. Although the targets were intended to heighten the contradictions, the explosions, while at times spectacular, only served to create more distance between the movement and the public at large. The heady fall mobilizations that generated expansive opposition to the war faded into the winter doldrums.

With the exception of the sexual encounters with Rachel, Frank seemed to be sleepwalking through his life. Even his H.E.P.P. class lost its verve during the winter term. He often plodded through the course material, unable to find the spark that had lit a fuse under the students in the fall. His counseling sessions were few and far between. Because of the winter weather, the tutoring lessons at the church had been suspended. His connections with the TCDAC and the Honeywell Action Project were on hold.

All of that changed on the evening of April 30.

As Frank turned on the small television set perched on a table in the corner of the living room of the house in North Minneapolis, he could not have anticipated what Nixon was going to say about a major policy change in the war. Nor could he have predicted the fury that the antiwar movement, especially on college campuses, would unleash. He begged Mary to come downstairs from her study to watch "Tricky Dick" once more make a complete dick of himself. Nixon was perspiring above his upper lip even before beginning his address to the nation. And then he spoke.

"Son-of-a bitch. I don't believe that asshole," Frank yelled at the TV.

"Please," Mary begged. "Stop your ranting. He can't hear you; only I can."

"But he just said that the U.S. is invading Cambodia although he called it an 'incursion.' He's widening the war, not shutting it down. Motherfucker! I've got to make some telephone calls and see what's going down."

Not wanting any part of Frank's frenetic revival, Mary climbed back up the stairs to her study and shut the door behind her.

The first person Frank tried to telephone was John Rider. Because he was now a leading voice on campus and a member of the Student Council, Rider was well placed to organize a demonstration in response to the Cambodian invasion. After getting a busy signal, he called David Marvinoff. When David answered, Frank didn't even bother to say "hello," but went right into a diatribe.

"Did you watch that bastard and his pathetic attempt to rally the American public, talking about the good old U.S. of A. as a 'pitiful, helpless giant?' You bet it's pitiful."

Calmly answering the frantic caller on the line, David told him about the emergency rally forming at the Old Federal Building downtown. Others were being notified as they spoke. Eager to join the protest, Frank hung up the phone and shouted upstairs to Mary that he was going to a demonstration downtown. Not hearing any reply, he rushed out the back door and jumped into the Corvair.

By the time he found a parking spot close to the Old Federal Building there were hundreds milling around, many with homemade signs saying "No Wider War; No War At All!" As he searched the crowd for familiar faces, he noticed Sarah Stark, a white-haired older woman who frequented many of the antiwar protests and was now the leader of the local Women Strike for Peace. There was also a group of Quakers, carrying multi-colored signs with the words, "War is Not Healthy for Children and Other Living Things." There was a contingent of students and street kids who had been occupying a site in Dinkytown to prevent the local stores from being bulldozed for a corporate fast-food franchise. Among that aggregation was Eileen Penny and Lamar Rice. While avoiding Eileen, Frank walked over to Lamar who greeted him with a Black Power raised fist.

"Hey, Lamar, how are you?" Frank inquired.

"Okay. But this is fucked up, man. So glad my lottery number is above 300."

"That's good news. By the way, how's your brother?"

"He's into some revolutionary shit. Don't see him much anymore, but when I do he's always packing. I think the murder of Fred Hampton and Mark Clark by the pigs in Chicago back in December really freaked him out. For me, I just don't wanna even deal with a gun."

"Me neither although I understand why your brother and other young Blacks want to take up arms and protect themselves."

"I guess that makes sense. It's just not my thing."

"I hear you," Frank said over his shoulder as he searched the crowd for his comrades. Walking away from Lamar, Frank paused to give the fist salute. Lamar raised his arm and smiled.

Frank tried to make out where his fellow radicals were. He finally located David, Bob Sagan, and Dale Coffee from SASS. He joined in their circle.

"Now's the time for a student strike," advocated a breathless Bob.

"Hell," David said, "We should call for a general strike! What better day to begin such a strike than May 1?"

Frank didn't share David's enthusiasm about the possibility of a general strike. He was just hoping for the campuses to mobilize. When John and another group of students showed up, they were already discussing a strike at the "U." Plans for a rally tomorrow in front of the Coffman Memorial Union were already in motion. Frank offered to go to the TCDAC office to produce flyers calling for a student strike. Rider assured him that such leaflets were being run off as they spoke.

The next day and for several days after colleges around the country erupted in opposition to the widening war. Hundreds of campuses shut down in student strikes, targeting, in the process, college ROTC buildings. In some instances, those symbols of the war club were torched. When the wooden ROTC structure was set on fire at Kent State, the Ohio Governor ordered the National Guard to that campus. On May 4th, the Guard opened fire on student protestors and bystanders, killing four and injuring scores of others.

Frank was standing in the shadows at the side of Coffman Memorial Union where students had been gathering for several days in anticipation of a student strike and occupation of the student center. Listening to a small transistor radio for news of the demonstrations, he was startled by the news flash of the deaths of students at Kent State. Pushing his way to where a speaker's stand and microphone was, he grabbed John Rider, who was addressing the crowd, to relay the information about Kent State. When John made the announcement about the killing of students on that Ohio college campus, the audience gave a collective groan. Some students wept openly while others started shouting, "Strike! Strike! Strike!" Those calling for a strike swept into Coffman Union, determined to occupy the building.

Frank and Bob Sagan decided to act as a two-person scouting party and go around to the back of the Union in order to locate another opening for the occupation. They split up, each heading in the opposite direction with the intention of meeting up behind the building. As Frank rounded the corner at the back, he ran smack into a half-dozen or so Minneapolis police.

"Well, well, look what we have here," said one of the oversized cops, "a long-haired hippie just itching for a fight."

Before Frank could turn and run, several of the police jumped on him, knocking him to the ground. For good measure, one of the cops rammed his baton into Frank's side, eliciting a scream of pain from the pummeled protestor.

"Did this little baby just call out for his 'mama?'"

Frank was yanked to his feet. When his arms were pinned behind him, he once again howled about the injury.

"Take him over the to the police van before this crybaby wets his pants."

As one cop clapped on handcuffs, another led him over to an area where the police vehicle was parked. Frank was shoved inside. Next to him was a young man, slumped over and bleeding profusely from his head. With his hands bound behind him, he was unable to do anything to stop the flow of blood other than calling out for a doctor to help the badly wounded kid next to him.

"Don't worry about that scratch," said a square-jawed detective. "They'll deal with that at the jail."

Not waiting around for any other beaten-up demonstrators, the police van took off with a blasting siren. Arriving at the downtown jail, Frank was separated from the blood-splattered young man and herded into a cell that contained two other disheveled victims of police brutality. He recognized one of them from SASS.

"Jesus, what happened to you guys?" he asked.

"We were just grabbed off the street by two cops who claimed we were disturbing the peace. Then, they pounded us into the back seat of their cop car. And here we are."

Frank tried calling out to get someone to give him his one phone call. One of the jailers showed up and escorted Frank from the cell to a phone. Hoping that Mary would answer and not be too angry about his arrest, Frank dialed his home number. Mary picked up.

"Don't be too upset, but I'm in jail."

"What?" she cried out. "What did you do?"

"Nothing. The cops just wanted to kick around some of the protesting students and I happened to wander into their lair. Can you get me an attorney? I want to get out as quickly as possible and have a doctor look at my ribs. I think one of them is broken."

"Oh, my god, Frank. I'll call Vince."

"Not Vince."

"Don't argue with me. He's with his Dad's powerful law firm now. I'm sure as a favor he'll do this *pro bono*."

"Maybe, but maybe he'll just throw the case out of spite."

Before Mary could counter his cynicism about Vince, the jailer took the phone out of his hands.

"Time's up. It's back to your cell, buddy."

When he got back to his cell, the other two were gone. Massaging his side, he slowly slid down onto the floor and passed out. He was startled awake when the jailer kicked his running shoe on his right foot and told him in a laconic tone of voice that his attorney was waiting to see him. Frank was escorted to a small room where Vince Bourgeois sat, spiffily attired in a dark suit with a brightly colored paisley tie. The attorney rose to shake his hand, but Frank rebuffed the outstretched arm.

"It hurts to pick up my right arm. I think they broke some of my ribs."

"Boy, that's not what the cops say. They've charged you with assaulting an officer, a felony."

"What the fuck! They beat the shit out of me." He was livid with indignation.

"Settle down. That's usually a tactic the police use when they want to cover up their own malfeasance. We can sue them for police brutality and they'll probably drop the charge or add some other misdemeanor, like disturbing the peace, to the other one."

"What other one?"

"Lurking."

"What the hell is 'lurking?'"

"It's an arcane statute that's used primarily against the homeless and disproportionately on Blacks who the cops roust on the street."

"Well, I'm not homeless, at least not yet, unless Mary is so pissed that she throws me out of the house. So, does that make me an honorary Black?"

"No way, white boy. You're still going to be treated as a privileged middle class white man when we get to court and I plead your case."

Although reluctant to grant Vince any gratitude, Frank had to admit that he was lucky to have representation from someone with the clout of a well-known name and a well-connected law firm.

"Thanks for doing this," Frank reluctantly offered.

"Just go home. See the doctor and get a medical report on your injuries. Get some sleep and I'll see about expediting this whole process. And by the way, Mary posted bail already. So, you'll be free to go after we finish here."

"Can you give me a ride home?"

"Sure. I've already wasted much of the day."

Vince knocked on the door to let the jailer know he had finished with his client. Trailing behind the two of them, Frank, still rubbing his side, followed his lawyer to the desk where he collected the pocket items, keys and the like, that had been taken from him at his jailing.

When Vince dropped Frank off at his house, Mary was in the living room in her grandma's old rocking chair, the one family relic that her parents had passed on to their only daughter. Trying to avoid Mary's livid look, he sheepishly cast his eyes downward to where her size four shoes propelled the rocker back and forth in a resolute motion.

"Sorry for this mess. Thanks for arranging for Vince and my bail."

She just sat there fuming for the next few minutes. He was reluctant to say anything more until she spoke up first.

"Call the doctor and see how quickly you can get an appointment. Then, let me see your injury and what I can do for it."

Once again, he thanked her.

"I don't think I want to hear any more thanks. And I certainly don't want to have to listen to any more apologies for your crazy political capers."

He resisted responding. This was not the time or place to begin another argument about his principled political stands. What he saw as engaging in justified rebellion, she had reduced to "political capers." At this point, he could not determine if the physical pain he was suffering from his injury was as intense as the psychological sting he endured from her criticism. Better leave this to another day, he thought. For now, maybe showing her his bruises would mollify her anger and frustration with him. Lifting up his shirt, Frank motioned to Mary to look at his wounds. Beyond a suppressed yelp when she gazed at the black and blue marks on his right side, his wife sat back in the rocker, picked up a book, and just shook her head.

As a concession to his injuries, she did drive him to the doctor's office where the examination revealed one broken rib for which nothing could be done other than writing up an extensive report on his physical state. He telephoned Vince after he got back home to tell him of the doctor's report. Mary excused herself and left to teach her class at the trade school. He was left alone to rest on the couch, nursing his wounds and his pride.

After a brief nap, Frank went into the kitchen to make some lunch for himself. Before he could open the refrigerator door, the phone rang. It was an animated Ted on the line, reporting on what had just transpired at the Dinkytown occupation. Now that he was the editor and chief reporter for the most widely distributed and read "underground" weekly newspaper in the Twin Cities, *Revolutionary Waters*, whose masthead – "All revolutionaries must be able to swim in local waters" - combined Ted's idiosyncratic brand of Maoism and Populism, he had toned down his use of hallucinogenic drugs. He had written down the preliminary elements of a story he would publish in *Revolutionary Waters*, highlighting how a large phalanx of Minneapolis police had charged into the occupied spaces and battered their way through unarmed and defenseless kids. The worst part, he related breathlessly to Frank, was that one cop had fired his weapon on a young Black male who was left to bleed to death while the rest of the ferocious force cleared the area.

"Oh, my god. Do you know the name of the Black kid?"

"I think it was something like Tamar or Lamar Rice."

Frank dropped the phone. Picking it up with a bitter guttural growl, he told Ted that Lamar Rice was a sweet kid who was not a threat to anyone.

"Well, the cops are already saying he had a weapon in his hand. All the eyewitnesses I talked to claimed that the only thing the kid might have been holding is a spatula since he was cooking up some hamburgers on a grill in the alley in the back of the shops. What a fuckin' tragedy."

It wouldn't be the last tragedy involving young Blacks and racist police. A week and a half after Lamar was murdered, city and state cops in Mississippi killed two Jackson State students and injured twelve others. The Minneapolis cop who shot Lamar wasn't charged. Instead, he was exonerated and awarded a desk job for his meritorious duty. No one was ever charged in the Jackson State killings.

At the end of May, Frank got a reminder about why the Black Panthers called the police an "occupying army" in the inner city neighborhoods around the country. In the middle of the day as Frank was reading in his living room, several cop cars screeched to a halt in front of the house on the opposite side of the street. With guns drawn, they bounded up the stairs while a helicopter hovered overhead. Two cops came out of another car with a battering ram that they used to smash down the front door. While those two remained outside, the others rushed inside.

Watching this scene unfold, Frank was first frightened and then outraged by this police raid of a neighbor's house. Without thinking, he charged out of his own place and shouted over to one of the cops.

"What the hell's goin' on?"

With his weapon drawn, one of the cops stepped in Frank's direction, hollering, "Get the fuck back in your house!"

Not wanting to argue or to provoke this adrenaline-driven armed menace, Frank retreated. After a brief time, the cops left. A shattered door remained. Later Frank found out that this was a drug bust on the wrong address. According to his neighbor, the police never paid to fix the door even though his attorney filed a claim for restitution.

Forty-Two

SUMMER 1970

Vince had made good on his claim. The charge of "assaulting a police officer" was almost immediately dropped after the filing of a civil law suit alleging police brutality, accompanied by the requisite photographs of Frank's injuries and the doctor's report. Frank appeared in court wearing a polyester suit that stood out in its garishness, especially in contrast to the stylish tailored outfit worn by his lawyer. While Vince's suit clearly carried the day as a fashion statement, the rumpled jacket of the prosecutor, the Ichabod Crane lookalike, drew a withering look from the black-cloaked judge. The decision rendered by His Honor, a friend of Vince's father, added another demerit to the prosecutor's case when the "lurking" charge was dismissed. Frank received a thirty-day probation sentence for disturbing the peace. Elated with the outcome, he thanked Vince and left the courtroom with Mary.

Neither said anything on the drive back home. Once Mary parked the Corvair, she entered the house not even waiting for

Frank. When he finally trudged inside, he could hear Mary rocking back and forth in the living room. She was inexplicably crying. With some hesitancy, he asked why she was upset.

"It's over."

"Yeh, I know," he acknowledged, reflecting on the additional strain this trial had put on an already tenuous marriage. "But now that the trial's over now, maybe we can do some repairing of our relationship."

"I can't. I won't. I'm filing for divorce."

Shaken by the news, Frank joined Mary's quiet weeping. He feared that she might take an irrevocable step like this, but hoped that maybe there was something he could do to rekindle the flame that he had helped extinguish. The marriage had dissolved like a candle that melted without even a hint of a wick left. It was, indeed, over.

"What do you want me to do?" he inquired between sobs.

"You can stay here until you find another place to live. I'd like to remain in this house because of its proximity to where I teach and the garden."

She had truly nurtured that plot of land in the backyard, giving it all the attention and love she could not offer him any longer.

"I'll look around. I'll try to be out by the end of this month."

After the initial shock and immediate grief over the break-up, Frank had to admit later that week that he felt relieved. He was free now to engage in the most radical actions without having to worry about Mary's feelings and the fallout it would cause. Perhaps, the feeling of freedom he experienced had a connection to his desire for an even stronger commitment to rebel. Recalling a passage from Camus that "the only way to deal with an unfree world is to become so absolutely free that your very existence is an act of rebellion," Frank embraced that freedom and its concomitant rebellion.

Forty-Three

MID-MAY TO LATE JUNE 1970

Back in mid-May before the trial and the dissolution of his marriage, Frank plunged into student strike activities throughout the Twin Cities. He accompanied Robert Bly, the Minnesotan poet, antiwar activist, and draft resistance supporter, to Hamline College, a small liberal arts institution of higher learning in St. Paul, where Bly recited his Vietnam War verses. In additional remarks, Bly noted that the "Vietnam War is a continuation of the Indian wars. We just ran out of Indians."

But there were still any number of Indians residing in Minneapolis. Among them were the Bellecourt brothers, Clyde and Vernon, and Dennis Banks, all urban members of the Ojibwa nation, who founded the American Indian Movement (AIM) in 1968. By the spring of 1970, AIM leaders, like Clyde Bellecourt and Dennis Banks, were participants in various antiwar demonstrations in the Twin Cities where they made the connection between the massacres at My Lai and Wounded Knee.

On the University of Minnesota campus, the student strike permeated all of the routines of academic life. Faculty organized as a strike committee, pushing through the removal of the ROTC from the campus. Employees at the "U" also banded together in a militant alliance of university workers, finding a variety of ways to encourage and enable the strike. Coffman Memorial Union became "Strike Central" with ad-hoc committees occupying offices and plotting strategies and tactics to keep striking students involved. One of those activities was a mock graduation ceremony with thousands of students jammed into Northrop Auditorium. Frank led the draft card turn-in with a defiant speech on resistance. His rant included ripping up the 4-F certificate he had been sent as a way of ridding the Selective Service System of a student pest. He wasn't going to be brushed off so easily. Instead, he continued to buzz around, busy as a bee and as pesky as a mosquito.

Elsewhere in Minnesota, students engaged in short strikes, teach-ins, and turning in draft cards. When forty draft cards from St. Olaf College in Northfield arrived at the TCDAC office, Frank was there to help his fellow draft resisters process this act of resistance.

The draft card turn-ins at St. Olaf and the "U" led to a reconsideration of planning for an action at certain Selective Service offices in at least two cities in Minnesota. Joining with the crew at TCDAC, Frank, Dan Whitman, John Rider and Jim Penny, was Dale Coffee of SASS. It was Frank who initiated the conversation.

"Given the momentum from the student strike and the resistance raids around the country at draft boards, I think it's time to choose some places to attack. I want to propose

Moorhead and Winona, both small cities but with contacts that might be able to help us."

Dan responded with some skepticism. "I haven't heard from Fred in the last several months. I know there was another foray into Mount Doom, the missile site in North Dakota where he got arrested and jailed for trespassing. I got a letter from Stan saying Fred was okay, but recuperating from the whole affair. When I tried to call up there, I never was able to get through. So, not sure what kind of contact we have with Fred. Maybe we can use the connection at Concordia College if we decide to go through with this and if Moorhead is one of the locations. I'm just not prepared to risk an arrest and leave the TCDAC in the lurch."

Frank was quick to counter Dan's pessimism about the repercussions of a raid. "Look, if we do enough research and go at a time when people would be distracted, such as the evening of July 4th, I can almost guarantee we can get away with it."

"There are no guarantees," Dan glumly pointed out.

Jim chimed in with his own reservations. "While I'd consider doing such an action, I'm not sure it makes sense to do it on July 4th. My sister got arrested at the Dinkytown occupation and I'm a little reluctant to leave Minneapolis while the trial is going on."

"Don't worry. She and the arrested others have all kinds of legal and public support. Besides, if you and I go as a pair to Winona, we can be in and out of the draft office in no time."

Eager to be one of the draft raiders now that he had dropped out of his grad program and taken on more responsibility for SASS, Dale glanced over to where John was listening intently. "I think John and I could do the Moorhead action. Besides ever since the Muskrat 44 raid in St. Paul, I've been dying to rifle through Selective Service files and fuck up the system."

"I'd like to go to Moorhead," John retorted. "Not only to be part of a dynamic duo with Dale, but to find out what's happened to Fred. So, maybe we could go up there for a week or so and crash at Concordia with some of those contacts I made previously."

"C'mon, Jim." Frank begged. "You can give me a birthday present. Instead of lighting candles on a cake, we can light up draft files. What do you say?"

"Okay, as along as we just get in there and get out quickly."

"Of course. We'll have to go there maybe a week before and do some reconnoitering. Don't we have a contact at St. Mary's College in Winona, Dan?"

"Yeh. After the Cantonsville Nine and Milwaukee Fourteen action, a few of the Catholic radicals at St. Mary's called here and asked to have someone come down and talk about the draft. We never got around to doing that, but I think I still have the name and telephone number."

"Great," Frank enthusiastically observed. "So, with John and Dale journeying to Moorhead and Jim and I doing a hit-and-run number in Winona that would make us the "Minnesota Four." And if we can agree to do it on July 4th, it will also have symbolic meaning as a statement of our rebellion against a tyrannical system."

"Forget the symbolism," Dale said as he stood up to stretch. "I'm more interested in destroying draft files. The sooner, the better. The more, the merrier."

Jim's sour expression suggested there was nothing "merry" about the raids on these designated Selective Service offices. Seeing Jim's downcast look, Frank took him aside for a pep talk.

"You and me together. We can do this. There's no reason to worry, Jim. I'll be driving in my trusty Corvair. It will be late at night. We'll case the place a week before during the day and have some local help. It will all go smoothly."

"I'm not so sure. What if there's an alarm?"

"You can disable it with your trusty axe. How about June 28th as our day to check out the scene down there?"

"Well, I guess it seems you've got it all planned. June 28th it is."

Forty-Four

On the Friday morning that Frank drove his Corvair to Jim's apartment in South Minneapolis, the long-range B-52 Stratofortress bombers were back at their airbase in Guam after dropping their load of five-hundred-pound bombs on Cambodian targets. Nixon's secret air war, initiated in 1969, would remain relatively unknown to the American public and even to the U. S. Congress until 1973. By then, tens of thousands of innocent Cambodians were killed and hundreds of thousands were displaced. In the process, the neutral government of Prince Sihanouk was replaced by a right-wing coup in the service of U. S. military and political interests.

Unaware of the carpet-bombing of Cambodia but fully aware of the ongoing war in Southeast Asia and the perpetuation of the Selective Service System, Frank and Jim were now on the road to Winona to do the reconnoitering for their July 4th raid on the local draft board office. The Corvair snaked along the highway bordering the Mississippi River as it headed south and east to a city that had been, up until the mid-nineteenth century, an eastern outpost of the Sioux Nation. Settled first by New England Yankees, then by immigrant Germans and Poles, Winona was on June 28, 1970 a small town of around 26,000 people. Among those residents was their contact at St. Mary's College, Ron Pulaski.

"Who is this guy we're supposed to meet at the local Catholic college?" queried Frank.

Jim took out a piece of paper from the back pocket of his jeans containing the name and brief bio of the former student at St. Mary's who would be their guide. "His name is Ron. He's just graduated and waiting to go to Chicago to join with the Catholic Workers there."

"Sounds like a pretty committed guy. I'm assuming you've got the address of the local Selective Service office on that same piece of paper."

"Shit! I forgot to write it down. I'm sure Ron will know the exact address since he's been part of a number of demonstrations in front of whatever building it's in."

Not only did Pulaski familiarize Jim and Frank with where the local draft board office was, he also gave them an extended tour of Winona and its surroundings. He was especially insistent that the two Minneapolis draft resisters climb to the top of Sugar Loaf, a river bluff in Winona, where they could see across to Wisconsin and view the Mississippi as it flowed by on its long route to the city of New Orleans and out to the Gulf of Mexico. Exhausted by the climb and overwhelmed by Ron's non-stop commentary, including his own family history that went back several generations, Frank and Jim were relieved when he exited the Corvair back at St. Mary's and they could return to Minneapolis.

After dropping off Jim, Frank drove to Dinkytown to check out a basement studio apartment not far from the rooming house where he resided when he first arrived in Minneapolis. He signed a thirty-day lease to rent the rather dank and dingy dwelling, fulfilling the promise to Mary to move out before the end of the month and consigning himself to an underground existence. Before leaving Dinkytown, he stopped to eat dinner at the little Japanese restaurant that had been a favorite of his during his previous tenancy.

Forty-Five

She was not going to eat dinner before the picketing of Camille Paglia's talk at *The Rebel* Bookstore. She was too nervous. Lacing up her Doc Martens Orchid Purple Pascal boots, Ruth wished that Eileen had stayed a little longer in Toronto. She had left a few weeks ago after receiving her doctorate for the Twin Cities and a great job offer to oversee some new programming at a number of women's shelters. In Eileen's absence, Ruth plowed ahead with recruiting some of the radical feminist sisters among undergrad and grad students at the University of Toronto. The recruitment on campus had led to some ferocious debates about Paglia's work, what constituted radical feminism, and, of course, the whole issue of free speech. As a devotee of McKinnon and Dworkin, she dismissed those who would cloak themselves in absolutist notions of free speech at the expense of the safety and sanctity of women. She knew that words hurt and injured women and rationalizations of male supremacy under any guise, including those of the pyrotechnical rhetoric of Paglia, were harmful and had to be confronted as such.

Ruth had arranged to meet her fellow picketers on Bathurst, just a few blocks away from the target of their demonstration. She would walk there by herself on this balmy early Friday evening in her comfortable but sturdy shoes. Grabbing her hand-lettered sign with the message "End Rape Culture" printed in bold black capital letters, she exited her Queens Park studio apartment and ran down the several flights of stairs out onto College Street, heading over to Bathurst. When she met up with her comrades, the dozen determined women also carried homemade signs. Together, they marched off to *The Rebel* Bookstore.

Ruth had planned for the protest to begin at 7 P.M., a half hour before Paglia was scheduled to speak and maybe early enough to dissuade potential audience members from attending this book talk by the notorious anti-feminist. When the owner of the store heard the commotion outside and saw the gaggle of picketers congregated out front, he hurried to find out why they were there and what he could do to prevent any disruption from taking place.

"What's going on here?" he asked.

Ruth stepped forward. "We're here to protest this bookstore's sponsorship of someone who we believe has no understanding of the pervasive nature of rape culture. In fact, her writings make light of the efforts of radical feminists like us to end rape culture."

The owner, a fifty-year-old bearded gentleman, was taken aback. "I think you've misread Paglia's writings. She's not dismissive of those who want to stop this kind of violence against women."

Ruth adamantly held both her physical and political position. "Spoken just like a man with no real understanding of feminist issues."

"That's not fair. You know nothing about me."

"Nor do I wish to know anything about you. So, just let us demonstrate without any harassment from you."

"I think you are doing the harassment. Why don't you come inside and listen to what Paglia has to say and then ask whatever questions and make whatever comments you want?"

"That's a nice patronizing gesture," scornfully Ruth responded.

"Ok. At least back up and allow my customers the right to enter or exit." As the owner said this, he raised his hands and motioned for Ruth to move. Viewing his gesture as a prelude to being pushed aside, she instinctively resorted to her kickboxing training and let loose with her right leg smashing him in the chest. He fell backwards, hitting his head on the cement pavement. As he started bleeding from his ear, Ruth immediately dropped to the ground where he lay unconscious.

"Please, someone call an ambulance," she pleaded with her comrades.

A woman dashed out of the bookstore. Seeing her husband lying unconscious with blood seeping from a head wound, Joan was distraught.

"What happened?" she yelled out to the crowd, not noticing the young woman kneeling next to her.

"I didn't mean to hurt him. I thought he was going to assault me. It was an accident," the young woman stammered.

Joan angrily responded, "He's a goddam pacifist. He wouldn't attack you or anyone for that matter." Now looking up at those gathered round, she again repeated her request for getting medical help. Just at that moment a vehicle from the Toronto Ambulance Service pulled up in front of the Bathurst bookstore. A woman paramedic was first on the scene, followed by her male partner. Administering immediately to the unconscious man on the ground, she staunched the bleeding.

"We're going to have to take him to the hospital right now."

"Can I ride with you? I'm his wife."

"Yeh, okay. Let me and my partner get him on the stretcher and then you can sit by his side on the way to the hospital."

Ruth was obviously in agony as she asked the female paramedic, "What hospital are you taking him to."

"Toronto General. Are you related to him?"

"No, but I'm maybe at fault for the accident," Ruth replied.

"Well, that's something the police will have to investigate."

Joan saw how shaken this young woman was. Trying to calm her as well as herself, she told Ruth that she would not press charges.

Ruth started to sob. "Can I please go to the hospital and sit with you? I need to make sure that he's going to be alright."

Joan looked into the tearing eyes of this stranger who had caused this awful incident and took pity on her. "Yes. If they give you any hassle at the hospital, just say you're our daughter."

"Thank you. What's your name and his?"

"I'm Joan Roth. He is my husband, Frank."

Ruth repeated the names of Joan and Frank Roth as a rehearsal for any inquiry at the hospital about her identity. Turning to her fellow picketers, she explained why she was leaving the group and gave her picket sign to another one of the other feminist protestors. Striding quickly in the direction of Toronto General Hospital, she hoped that she wouldn't be turned away.

By the time Ruth reached the hospital, Frank and Joan were in the Emergency Room. Frank's eyes kept on fluttering open and shut. He lay under Joan's worried gaze without uttering a sound. The resident doctor swooped in, glanced at the chart with Frank's vitals, and then started to examine the patient.

"Is he going to be alright?" she queried.

"We won't know until we run a number of tests, including a CT scan. In the meantime, please wait in the lobby. Someone will inform you about his condition once we have a better sense of what's going on."

Joan made her way to the large lobby. Curled up in a corner chair was the young woman from the bookstore protest. As Joan approached the now shoeless blonde, Ruth stood up.

Repeating the exact words Joan posed to the emergency room resident, she breathlessly inquired, "Is he going to be alright?"

"I hope so. I was told to wait here in the lobby while they do some tests and then someone would let me know."

Ruth was shaking, a combination of her anxiety, remorse, and lack of food. She remained standing until Joan took a seat next to the corner chair. Then, Ruth slumped back onto the bland institutional green sectional. Her face almost matched the color of the chair.

Noticing how pale Ruth looked, Joan felt compelled to ask, "How are you doing?"

"Still dazed. I'm so sorry. Can you forgive me?"

"I can. And I hope Frank will do the same."

They sat in silence for some time. When Joan spotted the resident doctor from the Emergency Room peering around the lobby, she hurried over to talk to him. Ruth remained plastered to the chair, fearful of any number of dreaded possibilities. Joan returned to tell her of these alarming developments.

"They're going to have to induce a coma because of the swelling of his brain. He'll be out for at least a week, but they think they'll be able to bring him out of the coma and do any repair that may be necessary."

Ruth was thunderstruck. Her body literally twitched with the news. Joan calmly advised her to go home, eat, and get some rest. She would stay in the hospital until Frank was put in a coma. Once he was stabilized, Joan would also leave to get some sleep and return in the morning.

"Can I come visit you and Frank in the hospital tomorrow?"

"Of course, just remember to let them know that you're our daughter."

The next morning when Ruth returned to the hospital after a restless night's sleep, she was given the room number for Frank Roth without any questioning beyond the obligatory one about her relationship to the patient. She was in such a rush to get to the hospital that she hadn't bought the flowers that she intended would be a down payment on the expiation of her guilt. Somehow, she would have to find other gifts to give to the Roths.

Peeking into Frank's assigned private room, Ruth observed Joan sitting beside his bed, holding his limp hand.

"Is it okay if I come in?'

"Please do."

Taking one of the folding chairs by the monitors hooked up to Frank's various body parts, Ruth settled across the bed from Joan.

"Did you get some sleep," Joan asked solicitously.

Lying in order to allay Joan's concerns, Ruth answered with a forced smile and a rather hollow, "Oh, yes. How about you?"

"Not much. I didn't leave the hospital until 4 A.M. and then was back here at 8 A.M."

"Can I get you anything? I was going to bring flowers, but forgot. If there's something I can do now, just let me know."

"That's so kind of you," Joan sincerely said. "Nothing now other than telling me a little about yourself."

Ruth hadn't intended to say much about herself, but Joan's request was so heartfelt that Ruth had to comply with the request.

"Well, I was born in Minneapolis in 1971. My Mom was a grad student at the University there about to get her doctorate in American Studies."

Joan inadvertently squeezed Frank's hand as she sat stunned in the chair. Before Ruth could continue her autobiographical remarks, Joan asked what was her mother's name.

"My mom was Mary Browne. I'm her only daughter. Never met my birth father."

Joan was now in a minor tizzy. She didn't know how much to reveal about her husband. So, she let Ruth continue.

"Anyhow, my mom passed last year from breast cancer."

"I'm so sorry for your loss."

"Thank you. I guess her death was part of the incentive to start grad school here at the University of Toronto."

Before Ruth added any additional information, Joan felt compelled to divulge the secrets that Frank had told her and which she had never previously disclosed, even to her parents and closest friends. However, she needed to ask one question of Ruth, a question that would trigger the revelations about her husband that she had harbored for almost twenty-five years.

"Do you know if your mother was married and what the name of her husband was?"

Ruth thought this was an odd question, but answered it without hesitation, "Franklin Roosevelt Goodman."

"Oh, my god. I don't believe it." It took a minute or so before Joan could shake off her surprised disbelief and gain her composure. She now looked warmly into the reddened eyes of this young woman, reclining in a chair on the opposite side of a hospital bed where a husband and now, perhaps, a father lay.

"My husband's real name is Franklin Roosevelt Goodman. He changed it to Roth when he married me in 1972."

Ruth was dumfounded. "What? How is this possible?"

"Didn't your mother tell you about him and how he fled to Canada at the end of August in 1970?"

"No, she always insisted that the man who was my father was just part of a brief romance. I never pressed her on this matter. I didn't even know she was married until after her death when I found the license locked away with some legal papers."

Then, Ruth turned even whiter than her blonde hair. 'Oh, Jesus, I may be responsible for his death, my own father's death."

Releasing her grip on Frank's hand, Joan walked over to the other side of the bed. She enveloped Ruth's head into her comforting arms. Stroking the blonde hair, Joan let Ruth sob into her own heaving breasts.

"We have a lot more to talk about than I ever imagined," Joan delicately declared while still cradling Ruth.

Over the next week, as Joan and Ruth watched over Frank, they shared the intimate details of their lives. Ruth learned about Frank's courting of Joan and his work first at the University of Toronto bookstore before striking out on his own. Because of the success of her restaurant, the Homecooking Café, a popular lunch and dinner spot on Bathurst Street in the Jewish section of town, she was able to loan Frank some money to help open up *The Rebel* Bookstore. There were many other family secrets and confidential stories that Joan and Ruth shared during the week that Frank remained in a coma. By the time the doctors removed the anesthesia that was keeping him in a coma, the prognosis for his recovery was excellent. So, both women went home on the evening of July 4th, relieved and now bonded for life.

Early on the morning of July 5th, Frank finally awoke. The night nurse heard him screaming, "Run, Jim, run." He repeated the admonition a number of times before she was able to get to his bed, calm him down, and welcome him back to conscious life.

Forty-Six

JULY 5, 1970

"Run, Jim, run," he shouted. Hearing a distant siren, Frank did not want to risk being caught even though the noise could just be an ambulance on a 3 A.M. run. He quickly exited the door that they had jimmied open, not bothering to see if his partner was following him out the door and down the steps. At the bottom of the stairs, Frank looked up to see that Jim had tripped over some of the draft files they had thrown onto the floor. Now that the siren was even closer, he made a dash for the exit in the back of the building, hoping that Jim would be right behind him. With the siren piercing his ears, Frank no longer hesitated, but ran as fast as he could down the alley in the direction of where he had parked the Corvair.

As soon as he reached the car, he glanced back to see if Jim was in sight. Frank was breathing heavily. Paralyzed by fear and growing guilt, he stood next to the Corvair for only a short time before opening the door and starting the engine. Trying to avoid panic and stomping on the gas pedal, he maneuvered the car slowly through the darkness. When it sputtered to an unintended stop, he shouted out as loud as he could the magical incantation. The Corvair re-started. Relieved but still harried, he drove steadily towards the bridge that crossed the Mississippi to the Wisconsin side of the river. For some reason, he believed traveling on that route north would be safer. The deserted road helped calm his jangling nerves. He would continue on Highway 35 until he reached the bridge across the Mississippi to Red Wing, Minnesota.

He began debating whether it made any sense to return to his basement studio apartment. Would Jim now in custody confess that he had a partner in crime? Would the authorities be waiting for him at his residence? These doubts rattled around his brain as the line from the new Temptations song, "Ball of Confusion," punctuated the qualms about whether to return to Dinkytown. "Run, run, run, but you sho can't hide!" Maybe he should disappear into the woods for a while. He rejected that idea as absurd since he had no provisions and no camping equipment to withstand any of the elements. So, he would go back to his temporary home and seek the solitary solace of being an underground man.

By the time he reached Dinkytown, the day was beginning to dawn. Only a few early morning stragglers were out on the streets. Now exhausted, both physically and mentally, Frank parked the Corvair and slumped over the steering wheel for a moment to collect his troubled thoughts. Why had he abandoned Jim? Wasn't there enough time to turn back after seeing that Jim had fallen? It was these questions that would plague his mind for weeks, causing him to experience the kind of "hyperconsciousness" that Dostoyevsky identified as "a disease." For Frank, the malady was indeed a psychological one – a dis-ease from which he suffered that, in turn, led to a reappearance of insomnia.

He was tired and knew he needed to sleep. Yet, the small bed in the basement seemed more like a rack upon which he would be tortured rather than an inviting cushion of comfort. So, he decided to take a hot shower with the expectation that the warmth of the water might provide some soothing relief. Shedding his sticky clothes, Frank entered the skinny stall, turned on the water, and was met with a constant cold stream. There would be no consoling shower. After only a brief washing, he turned the handle to off and grabbed a towel that he wrapped around his waist.

He remembered that either he or Jim was supposed to call Dan and let him know what happened in Winona. Dan would also be hearing from John or Dale about the Moorhead raid. What would he say? How would he explain leaving Jim behind? It was with some trepidation that Frank picked up the telephone and dialed Dan's number.

The phone rang only once. Dan picked up. "Yeh. Who's this?"

Frank hesitated. Was he already paranoid about talking on the phone? Reluctantly, he announced himself. "It's me, Frank."

"Don't say another word. I already heard what went down in Winona. You can explain yourself later. Also, heard from Stan in Moorhead that the cops were tipped off and busted John and Dale even before they could enter the building housing the Selective Service facility."

Frank was despondent. "Should I come over to your place or go to the TCDAC office?"

"Neither. Just lay low for the next few days. We'll maybe talk at the end of the week."

"Okay." He hung up. Staring into the darkened space of his basement apartment, Frank consigned himself to exile as an underground man for the foreseeable future.

Forty-Seven

JULY 5, 1996

Recovering from the induced coma, Frank felt like he was returning from being an exile from his consciousness. He had no idea how or why he landed in the hospital with what the night nurse told him was a brain injury. He would rely on other medical staff to provide him with more details about his condition. In the meantime, he hoped that Joan would soon show up to lend a helping hand and succor his recuperation.

At that moment, Joan was at the hospital meeting with the neurosurgeon who oversaw her husband's treatment. He assured her there would be no permanent brain damage with the possible exception of some minor amnesia related to what transpired before he suffered the trauma to his head. Thanking him for his care and prognosis, Joan prepared herself to meet the newly awakened Frank Roth. Since Ruth planned to visit today, Joan would also introduce her as the daughter that Franklin Roosevelt Goodman never knew he had sired.

When Joan entered Frank's hospital room, he was sitting up in bed and sipping on some orange juice. The moment they saw each other, they burst into tears.

Frank spoke first. "Oh, my god, it's so good to see you. I missed you, but have no idea for how long."

Brushing his lips with hers, she told him the length of time he was in a coma. "I was here every day for that week, holding your hand and telling you the news of the day."

"I have no memory of any of that."

She picked up both of his hands and stared into his eyes. "For much of that time there was someone else who watched over you and kept me company."

"Who was that?"

"She'll be here shortly. I'll let her tell you."

Frank was intrigued, of course. He wondered who it could be. Joan's sister who lived in Montreal? Not likely. He stopped trying to guess and, instead, peppered Joan with questions about what had happened during the week that he was unconscious. She tried to spare him any information that would upset him, not wanting to add to the trauma he suffered. Besides, once Ruth arrived, there would be more than enough excitement for him to handle.

After an hour or so, a pretty young woman with blonde hair, blue eyes, and a large Adam's apple, not unlike his own protruding one, entered the room. She stood mesmerized by the sight of Frank, thinner and paler than when she last saw him as a conscious being. Joan invited Ruth to take a seat next to the bed. Once Ruth had positioned herself next to Frank, Joan started making the surprise introduction.

"Do you remember the last time you saw your first wife?"

Frank wasn't sure where this was leading and was guarded in responding because of the presence of this stranger. He hesitantly replied, "Maybe."

"You told me all of the intimate details of the last meeting. The signing of the divorce papers and the farewell fuck."

Frank blanched when she used that word, not because it was foreign to her vocabulary – Joan liberally applied it as a noun, verb, adjective, and adverb – but because it seemed so harsh, diminishing what had been a rather poignant, if decidedly incongruous, moment.

As she reminded him, "You left Minneapolis shortly thereafter. Fled to Canada and never looked back. Well, this person you see now at your side is the "look back." She's very likely the child that issued from your last convergence with Mary. This is Ruth Browne, born on May 25, 1971, nine months to the day after that fateful encounter with your wife."

The blood in Frank's head was pounding, raising his concern about another brain injury. What he had just been told clearly altered his consciousness. Too astonished to say anything, he offered his hands to Ruth. This time, instead of interpreting the outstretched arms as a threat, she took them gently in her own hands, kissing one at a time. And the weeping began for both of them.

Forty-Eight

MID-JULY TO AUGUST 29, 1970

He wept openly. Still ensconced in his basement apartment, Frank listened intently as Dan relayed the awful information about the repercussions following the arrests and jailing of Jim, John, and Dale. The tears were partly due to the guilt that tormented him as a consequence of the capture and imprisonment of his former comrades. His lack of sleep gnawed at his emotions, eating away at any peace of mind and enabling periodic bouts of self-pity.

Hunkered down in an underground existence, Frank infrequently left his self-imposed isolation. On rare occasions he would go to the neighborhood grocery store for provisions. As a diversion during an outing for food, he picked up the July 17, 1970 copy of *Life* magazine. After putting away the few groceries he had purchased, he started leafing through the pages of the glossy publication. One story with accompanying gruesome photographs assaulted his fragile sensibilities. Under the heading of "The Tiger Cages of Con Son" were pictures of mutilated South Vietnamese prisoners. Many of the 180 men and 300 women incarcerated there by the corrupt U.S.-sponsored government were student protestors, discovered by a U.S. congressional delegation jammed into 5x9 foot filthy cubicles, bound by leg irons, and rotting away from hunger and torture. Any sense of despair over his own situation was completely dispelled after viewing and reading about these Con Son tiger cages.

Unable to purge these photographs from *Life* from his mind, they soon merged with all the horrific images of the U.S. war on Southeast Asia. From the napalmed children to the My Lai massacre, from the dropping of anti-personnel fragmentation bombs to the burning of whole Vietnamese villages, from the bodies of those labeled Viet Cong, piled in mass graves, to the body bags being shipped back to the United States of nineteen-year-old draftees caught up in a war that made no sense to them and to an increasing majority of the American people.

And yet the war raged on, a war, like the Con Son prison camp, rooted in French colonialism of the 1880s that eventually led to the formation of anti-colonialist Vietnamese resistance, called the Viet Minh, under the leadership of Ho Chi Minh, who were given arms by the American OSS during WWII to fight against the occupying Japanese, only to be betrayed by the Americans when they aided the French in re-establishing its colonial regime, one that was defeated at Dien Bien Phu in 1954, the year that the Geneva Accords established a temporary border between North and South Vietnam, only to have the agreement subverted by the Eisenhower Administration, which put in place the dictator Ngo Van Diem whose repression of the anti-colonialist Vietnamese in the South led to the formation of the National

Liberation Front whose increasing spread in the South caused Kennedy to send in U.S. Special Forces that turned into more and more American troops being sent to their graves in an increasingly senseless and brutal war that resulted in millions of Southeast Asian deaths and injuries and against which millions of Americans protested, including greater and greater numbers of U.S. soldiers and sailors.

As Frank continued to hide away, more of those Vietnam Vets began organizing and demonstrating. Joined by other young soldiers in military bases in the U.S. and Germany, they expressed their opposition to the war in a variety of ways from writing petitions to editing newspapers to sit-ins and even to sabotage. Rebellions within the war club were a prime factor in Nixon's so-called Vietnamization program. Yet, withdrawing troops and trying to co-opt and cool down the student and military rebellions were unsuccessful. The resistance raged on.

And Frank raged on, mostly alone in his basement hideout, still fearful of being arrested. His fear was unwarranted since neither Jim nor John nor Dale confessed to another participant in the draft raids. Yet, his paranoia about his plight would lead to the decision to flee to Canada. He told only one other trusted person about his determined resolution. When Mary called him in late August, he revealed to her his plans during their encounter at her apartment. Returning to his soon-to-be-abandoned underground existence, he finalized all the necessary arrangements for his drive north. He crawled into the narrow bed hoping to get some needed sleep before his departure. Then, just before midnight the telephone rang. Barely awake, he answered mumbling, "Who is this calling so late?"

Epilogue

JULY 6, 1996 TO MAY 25, 2020

It took a little while for Frank to recover from his head injury. Another week in the hospital after the induced coma for additional tests and then rehab for any residual effects from damage to the brain occupied much of his time during the rest of the summer and into the early fall. During this convalescence, both Joan and Ruth were very solicitous of his condition. With their nurturance, by the late fall he was back at the bookstore. He reinstituted the Book Talks at *The Rebel* in 1998. As a concession to Ruth, he invited Andrea Dworkin whose 1997 anthology of her articles, *Life and Death*, was featured at the bookstore. Ruth got an autographed copy.

Ruth continued her graduate studies. She volunteered at a women's shelter in downtown Toronto. Her involvement at this facility with the staff and the residents provided data and stories that were integral to her dissertation on domestic violence.

With a Ph.D. in hand, she accepted an offer from the Sociology Department at Wayne State University. Her three-year contract as an Assistant Professor ran from the academic year of 2001 to 2004. She received an extension for another three years during which time she was awarded tenure as an Associate Professor.

Living in Detroit, she re-connected with Jane Rose. That friendship extended outward to other Black and white professional women in the metropolitan area. One important consequence of her contact with Jane was the adoption of an orphaned one-year-old Black child in 2003. Jane insisted that Ruth would be a perfect single parent without any "white savior" complex. Ruth named the child, Simone, after Simone de Beauvoir and Frank's grandfather, Sigmund. Ruth and Simone made numerous trips to Toronto where Frank and Joan doted on the precocious kid. While delighted with this wondrous child, neither of the grandparents was inclined to visit the United States.

In 2007 the University of Minnesota recruited Ruth for a prestigious endowed chair in Women's Studies and Sociology. She and Simone moved to Minneapolis where she purchased a beautiful three-bedroom tree-shaded house in Prospect Park, an upscale community adjacent to the University and the Mississippi River. Ruth enrolled her young daughter in public school where Simone flourished. A short time after the move, Ruth met a vivacious dark-haired set designer who worked at the Guthrie Theatre. They soon became a couple. Anne was a hit with Simone also and the three of them lived a fulfilling, if blinkered, life until Simone became a teenage rebel.

At the age of thirteen, Simone joined the Black Lives Matter protest of the police murder of Jamar Clark on November 15, 2015. All through high school, Simone engaged with BLM, becoming a coordinator of protests around police brutality and against gun violence. In the summer of 2016, she was part of the demonstrations that followed the murder of Philando Castile, another Black man shot by a cop. This time she convinced Ruth and Anne that they had to become active in the BLM campaign.

It didn't take much convincing for Ruth to support Simone when, as a sophomore in high school, she helped lead a walkout in solidarity with the national commemoration on March 14, 2018 of the one-month anniversary of the mass shooting in Parkland, Florida that killed seventeen students and staff. The survivors of that tragedy mobilized for a "March for Our Lives" in Washington, D.C. Simone, Ruth, and Anne joined the hundreds of thousands on March 24 who occupied the streets of the nation's capitol, listening to the moving testimony of the multi-racial youth who gave voice to demands to end gun violence.

When the three of them came to Toronto to spend time with Frank and Joan over the Christmas Break in 2019, they finally convinced the reluctant father and grandfather to come to Minneapolis in late May of 2020 for Ruth's birthday and Simone's graduation from high school. A month after the visit, Frank developed a dry cough. His muscles ached and he had a fever. Shortly after being sent by his primary care physician to the hospital Frank was diagnosed with a new infectious disease, Covid-19. The increasingly desperate treatments could not save his life. When a distraught Joan called Ruth to tell her that her dad had passed, Ruth was devastated, as were Anne and Simone. Ruth decided that she would not celebrate her birthday in 2020.

On that day, May 25, in South Minneapolis, a tall Black man walked into a convenience store. His name was George Floyd.

www.ingramcontent.com/pod-product-compliance
Lightning Source LLC
Chambersburg PA
CBHW061147210726
48294CB00006B/1604